Praise for *No Presents Please*

Winner of the Atta Galatta-Bangalore Literature Festival Lifetime Achievement Award

"The collection affirms Kaikini as one of the most influential writers today."

—NIKHIL GOVIND, *The Times of India*

"The jury was deeply impressed by the quiet voice of the author through which he presented vignettes of life in Mumbai and made the city the protagonist of a coherent narrative. The Mumbai that came across through the pen of Kaikini was the city of ordinary people who inhabit the bustling metropolis. It is a view from the margins and all the more poignant because of it. This is the first time that this award is being given to a translated work and the jury would like to recognize the outstanding contribution of Tejaswini Niranjana, the translator." —RUDRANGSHU MUKHERJEE, chair of judges, DSC Prize for South Asian Literature

"This Mumbai is not a distantly observed city. Kaikini is right there, in the midst of it, rubbing shoulders with his people, intuiting their lives and emotions through skin-touch." —SHANTA GOKHALE, *Mumbai Mirror*

"An insightful, illuminating, and powerful collection. Kaikini's evocative stories are infused with the body and soul of Mumbai . . . Kaikini is powerful and valuable as a documenter, a mapper of the city. But he is much more than that . . . He is an antenna, gathering up the city's dreams and hurt, bewilderment and rage, and transmitting them ever so gently back into the zeitgeist. The result is a gift worth receiving."

—TRISHA GUPTA, *Scroll*

"Dense with details and gentle observations, these stories explore the lives of people we see without seeing, every single day . . . Kaikini examines these small but brave lives with deep sympathy. He captures their voices with unerring humour; conjures up their world with exquisite precision; and recreates the strange blend of anonymity and intimacy that is so characteristic of this teeming megapolis by the sea."

—SHABNAM MINWALLA, *The Hindu*

"Kaikini is one of the foremost writers of short fiction in Kannada and the translation makes it evident that he is a master of the form."

—MK RAGHAVENDRA, *Firstpost*

"There are many arresting and haunting moments in Jayant Kaikini's *No Presents Please* . . . Kaikini uses his considerable talent to yoke together quotidian images to create a picture of Mumbai that's both exact and impressionistic."

—SANJAY SIPAHIMALANI, CNBC-TV18

"Very few writers have caught the absurdities, pathos, and comic turmoil that drive life in an Indian city today with the vibrancy of Jayant Kaikini."

—GIRISH KARNAD

"Jayant Kaikini's compassionate gaze takes in the people in the corners of the city . . . This is a Bombay book, a Mumbai book, a Momoi book, a Mhamai book, and it is not to be missed." —JERRY PINTO

"Like no other Indian writer, Jayant Kaikini brilliantly reveals the foundations of Mumbai concealed under its high-rises. Kaikini perceptively captures details from the inner lives of people who have become a part of Mumbai, a microcosm of India. Even the most ordinary happenings in these stories have traces of history in them, with little gestures evoking deep memories. The joys in routine chores from everyday lives, the unfading aspirations of innocent lives even in the face of the macabre—Kaikini unravels all of this with a subtle lightness. He captures the transformation Indian cities are undergoing, but not without recognizing the tussle between the worldviews of the village and the city."

—VIVEK SHANBHAG, author of *Ghachar Ghochar*

No Presents Please

No Presents Please

Mumbai Stories

JAYANT KAIKINI

Translated from the Kannada by
Tejaswini Niranjana

Catapult  New York

This is a work of fiction. All of the characters, organizations, and events portrayed in this novel are either products of the author's imagination or are used fictitiously.

ISBN: 978-1-948226-90-5

Cover design by Jaya Miceli
Book design by Wah-Ming Chang

Library of Congress Control Number: 2019952223

Printed in the United States of America
1 3 5 7 9 10 8 6 4 2

To all those orphaned and undelivered letters
lying in post offices, addresses unknown,
unable to return

CONTENTS

No Presents Please

INTERVAL

HERE, MANJARI SAWANT, AGED TWENTY, WITH UNREMARK-able features and skinny limbs, was sitting in front of the stuttering TV set in her neighbor's house in the narrow old Mahindrakar Chawl near the Naupada ice factory in Thane. There, Nandkishore Jagtap, alias Nandu, at-tendant in Malhar Cinema, as the first show drew to an end, stuck the torch under his arm, pulled aside the door curtain with a whirr so that the fight scene's back-ground score spilled into the lobby, went into the men's toilet to splash some water on his face, and stood there looking at himself in the mirror. That these two were planning to run away together early tomorrow was a fact nestling snugly in the dark, like the secret of a bud that had not yet blossomed.

For the last three years, in this theater, heroes of different complexions have kept saying to the heroine, "Let's run away somewhere," four times a day, until the crowded twenty-seventh week. Gazing into the hero's eyes, smiling coyly, the heroine runs through the fountains and into the upper stalls and disappears. Where does she go, melting into the night, never to be seen again, not even in one's dreams? In the lights that come up after the "happy ending," the hero's patched pants and their frayed edges appear to shine. Hurriedly, the hero rushes around turning off the lights for the next show. He shines his torch on tickets, to help those fumbling to find their seats. As the audience floats away into the enchanting world of the film, our hero selects the ceiling fan in the lobby under which he will nap, between the posters, behind the curtains where the theater owner's servants will not find him. When he dozes, a million heroines lose their bodies and minds and names in the glistening screen. In the dark, disembodied, they wander into the hero's dreams—"Here I am!" "Am I not here?"—they mob him, kiss him, stroke him. When the bell shrieks, the hero runs to the door, to let the flood of people out of their world of dreams, to count the ticket stubs, stroking his red comb that peeps out of his pocket. The girl runs into the rain without an umbrella, somehow reaches home to stand in front of her parents and her brother, shivering, saying sorry for returning late.

Three years ago, Nandu had left his home in Vidarbha and come to the magical city of Mumbai, and ever since he started working at the cinema hall, which was a

grain in that enormous city, Vidarbha had receded from
him. First, Nandu worked with the men who climbed
ladders to paste film posters on the walls, marveling that
they held the actresses' limbs and noses in their hands.
Soon he became the "battery torch boy," or usher, of
Malhar Cinema. The same city that had seemed from
the distance of Vidarbha like an unreachable star was
now within his grasp, with all its colorful shackles. It was
in the very tickets whose stubs he tore off. As though he
controlled the big dream and its billion sorrows, its de-
feats, its victories, and its songs, Nandu walked around
outside when the show was going on.

When a thousand people were sitting in the dark,
having offered themselves up to the screen, Nandu liked
to sit on a sofa outside and smoke a cigarette. When he
thought of how the second-run film had many scenes
missing from the reels, with the audience not knowing
even at the end who the real murderer was, this was
also fun. Amid these pleasures, she had entered, like one
more of them, when the afternoon show had ended.
She was running in and out of the cinema hall, looking
scared.

"What is it?" asked Nandu.

"Purse," she said.

Nandu switched on his torch and searched under the
seats of the upper stall. "Don't worry, it will be found.
Come tomorrow. I'll keep it for you," he said. He looked
again before the six p.m. show began. And just like in

a film, he found it. Standing between the heaps of old posters, he looked through the purse out of curiosity. A few ragged pieces of paper—four rupees in change, two hairpins, rubber bands, a packet of fennel seeds, a pack of bindis, and stubs of some old cinema tickets.

The next day she came in the afternoon, along with a small girl. "Didn't I tell you it would be found?" he said, handing the purse to her. She shrieked with happiness and hugged her little friend. After that Nandu always noticed her whenever she came to the theater. Because her friend had called her Manjari, Nandu knew her name. Once, he saw her going away because she hadn't been able to get a ticket. "Manjari," he called after her, and making her come back, he had managed to bring her a ticket from inside. He was always happy if she came to see a film on the day of its release. He had still not exchanged a word with her, nor had he bothered to find out anything more about her. When his friends said, on seeing her, "Here comes your maal," he would get very upset that they called her a "piece." She would never come straight to him. She never spoke to him. It was as though it was enough to see each other. Even when he prepared himself in advance, at the moment of speaking to her, he lost heart. Searching for him with her eyes, Manjari would disappear.

Heroes changed their clothes, changed their horses. Songs came easily to them. The heroines opened their arms wide and ran up the mountain to embrace the heroes. They vowed to be with them in life and death and happiness and sorrow. Manjari woke up at night to collect water for her family when the taps flowed briefly. Nandu waited for a new day. The street was full of film posters soaking in the never-ending drizzle. In the narrow houses, coal stoves burned. Sometimes Manjari's mother would open the cupboard, and stand looking at all her worldly possessions.

A few steel vessels gleam inside the cupboard. Two sets of new clothes amid mothballs. The cupboard fears the weddings of the future. If it's kept open too long, her father gets irritated. Aayi weeps. Once again the cupboard is locked. The old Diwali sky lantern nestles on top of it.

If someone invited them to a wedding, they would go early in the morning and leave only after dinner. If they were invited only for the evening meal, they would skip lunch so as to be all the more hungry for dinner. The hands that tried to stroke her as she passed were the hands on which she tied rakhis at Rakshabandhan. Her brother, who had yelled at his wife just ten minutes ago, was now mounting the woman, panting in the dark. Bound by all these circumstances, Manjari's breath seemed to loosen when she saw the freshness of the gleam in Nandu's eyes.

Nandu comes out of his den of film posters. His feet take him near Mahindrakar Chawl, where he lingers until afternoon. Perhaps she will come into the street to post a letter,

*to stand in the ration queue or to take the neighbor's child
to school. Once in a while their eyes meet. At other times,
Nandu returns to the theater for the matinee show. Beyond
this mutual exchange of glances, neither of them knows anything more.*

Once a film ran into its jubilee week. All the theater
staff got new clothes. The film stars came. Manjari of
Mahindrakar Chawl got a special pass that day. Placing
some burning coals on a plate, she ironed her blouse,
and made sure, by sprinkling water on it, that her string
of jasmine flowers stayed fresh. Half an hour before
the show, they met hurriedly between the parked cars.
He was to open Gold Spot bottles for the actresses. She,
on the other hand, wanted to take in the scene. In that
brief meeting, did their fingers touch? Was there a shy
laugh, wonder, a sweaty brow? He ran into the theater.
She went to seat E-28. They met again in the interval.
He was standing with a huge cup of ice cream. She kept
waiting for the stars who were now to come on stage.
He called her three times. Then she came up to him.
The handsome young man sitting next to her, was he
walking with her? No, he was going in another direction. She snatched the ice cream from him.

"How about you?"

"No, you have it," he said.

Looking at the beauties going past, she began to eat
the ice cream. He waited to see if she would give him a
spoonful. But she didn't.

"You can give me a spoon if you wish," he said softly. Either she did not hear him or she forgot to respond in the flurry of China silks—she emptied the ice cream cup. "Shall I get another one?" he asked.

Looking away, she said, "Yes."

He ran to buy another cup. This time she might give him a spoonful—he waited. Just then people started rushing back to their seats. So as not miss the heroines, she said she would eat her ice cream inside. Feeling strangely hurt, he went to the side of the stage, where the theater manager was shouting at everyone. Nandu stayed in the foyer until the show was over. Later in the rushing flood of people, he did not see her. He didn't search for her either.

The next day it rained. The drops dashed themselves against the windowpanes. There was a Malayalam film for the matinee, and he went inside to see it even though he didn't understand a word. The film was filled with plump women who aroused him. In the evening, he went near Mahindrakar Chawl in the rain, still lost in the film. She appeared. He felt a strange release. It was as though the moment anticipating the meeting or the moment right after was filled with a pleasure that the actual meeting did not have. "Come tomorrow," he said. He returned to the theater. Both of them began to weave their dreams again.

She will say "this," and then I will say "that." In reply, she will say "that."

He will hold my hand and thrust his lips forward, and I'll close my eyes and bend my head a little.

She turns over on her side as the rain beats down on the chawl. In the theater, he changes his clothes.

The posters talk:

"Why don't you buy a red T-shirt?"

"Yesterday I bought you a rose, but it faded . . ."

"You always eat in a restaurant—what fun it must be."

"When you watch a nice TV show in your neighbor's house, do you think of me?"

"Why do you wear those torn pants?"

"Wait and see. I'll start my own business."

NANDU WAS BORED WITH THE ROUTINE AT THE THEATER. Apart from life in Vidarbha or life at the Malhar, there must be so many other ways of living. He should leave this theater, with its reruns and repeat shows. But how and where, and why? Eating daily from roadside carts, placing his clothes under his mattress to press them, and being collared by those black market ticket thugs— Nandu wondered what he should do. Silently, Manjari gave him the inspiration to leave.

And similarly, Manjari, who kept patching her old clothes, and waited so eagerly for her father to bring home some mutton once a year, also began to think. She floated, drunk on thoughts of Nandu, hoping that through him she would get far more than this—sweeping, washing vessels, Sunlight bar soap, kerosene . . . In the warmth of her solitude, she saw a way out of this. But once in a while, neither could re-member the other's face and would panic.

"Let's run away."

Who said this first, they could not remember. But it was said.

"As soon as possible."

This, too, was said. While the words were being ut-tered, their resolve strengthened, and from that moment a new spirit filled them both.

The next morning, she was to meet him at Jambali Naka. And then they would go from there. Where? That they could decide tomorrow. And until that morning dawned there was the long night ahead. For Manjari, the night felt like the doorway to a new life. For Nandu, the night filled his limbs with renewed strength. Manjari put her only two good sets of clothes and a sari into her cloth bag and hung it by the hook over the mori. When she slipped out in the morning on the pretext of fetching milk, she would take the bag with her. Nandu made a heroic attempt to get back the ten rupees he had loaned the boy at the soda stall. His salary, received yesterday, was safe. Three hundred was enough to go away with. Then he would work in new businesses, work toward his own. The last show was now going on. Stills in the glass cabinets were star-ing out at the empty veranda. Nandu thought of the impossible possibilities awaiting him, and chafed. At her neighbor's place, Manjari remembered that she won't be there tomorrow, and watched all the shows on TV before going home.

At midnight, the show ended and the theater emptied out. Nandu took his torch out and searched under the seats. Like the waiting night, the darkened theater frightened him. He lay down in his corner.

At three a.m., Manjari wakes up, goes to ease herself at the mori, looks at the clock, and goes back to sleep. Nandu wakes at five a.m., has a bath, puts all his belongings into his bag, and leaves the theater. At the same time, Manjari leaves her house with her bag. Both of them wonder at the number of people out at that hour. Nandu reaches Jambali Naka early. He watches the vegetable trucks emptying themselves out at the market opposite. He looks at the people nodding sleepily in the milk booth queue. Manjari comes slowly toward him, as though limping. Looking around a little fearfully, Nandu smiles at her and says, "Let's have some tea."

They walked along the main road by the big lake. There were already a number of young people rowing little boats. As the cool breeze blew from the river, Manjari and Nandu, as though confounded by the infinite possibilities afforded by their freedom, walked fast, almost running. He stopped near a roadside tea stall.

"I'm hungry. I want to eat something too," she said stubbornly. So they walked to the restaurant near the station. They sat down at a table on the empty upper floor. Before the waiter could come to them, Nandu tried to pull Manjari toward him with his right arm, as though for courage. He couldn't do it right, and something poked him, her chain or an earring, he couldn't tell. They took forty minutes to finish their vada sambar, upma, masala dosa, and tea. As they ate, he kept looking at her. For some reason, her teeth looked very prominent. For one instant, he felt they had been sitting there for years, eating. "Eat quickly," he said.

In the middle of all this, Nandu did try to ask her a couple of times, "You do love me, don't you?" Manjari moved her head as though to say "Why talk about all this now?" At home, Mother would have woken by now. She might have sent Manjari's brother to look for her at the milk booth. Manjari finished her dosa hurriedly. Nandu went ahead of her to pay their bill at the counter.

Seeing a hawker with a heap of roses, Manjari said, "I want a flower."

"Later," said Nandu, going into the station to stand in the ticket queue. If he were setting out from Thane, Victoria Terminus seemed like a powerful force drawing him in that direction. Okay, he would go to VT first. He was sure that once he got there, new roads would open up. He had seen the Malayalis who sold foreign electronics in the tiny shops lining the side streets. Indistinctly, these thoughts began to encourage him. The ticket queue was a long one. When Manjari came near him, he said, "Stand away," in a soft growl. She moved away. He felt that all his heroes had pushed him into battle without any weapons. The posters clinging to each pillar of the station seemed to have let go of him.

Manjari was looking at the sherbet seller with his kala-khatta bottles at the station entrance, and saw a new dawn appear. A dawn that promised her an empire to replace her world of cleaning and washing. Standing like that, and looking out of the station, she seemed unrelated to this boy who stood in the ticket queue. She stood as though she had no connection either to the muddled dark world of theater dreams Nandu had left behind or to the Victoria Terminus universe lurking on the horizon. Nandu shook himself as though freeing himself from his dreams. Here, in Manjari's eyes, the new morning shone brighter and brighter. What more could Nandu do for her, now that she had freed herself from her worn-out family relations and the dirty mori?

Nandu had reached the counter. "Two VT," he said.

"Return?" asked the man.

"No, single," said Nandu.

He walked quickly to where Manjari was standing, put a ticket into her hand along with some money, said, "I'll just be back," and went inside the station. Once inside, he ran up the stairs and reached platform number six from the bridge over the tracks. The fast train to VT was slowly moving out of the station. Jumping down the steps, Nandu ran. Like lightning, he leaped into a compartment and clung to the pole. As soon as Nandu had gone into the station, Manjari walked into the street, as though filled with new strength. Plunging into a flower shop, she bought herself a rose. As she pinned it to her hair, she went swiftly to the long-distance bus depot a few yards away, and shoved her way into a bus bound for the industrial park without asking where it was going.

The town was full of flower shops. The town was full of film posters. Having given each other the stimulus to start a new life, Manjari Sawant and Nandkishore Jagtap now began to think of each other in their journeys, so as to keep the fear away.

"Madhyantara," 1986

CITY WITHOUT MIRRORS

Satyajit was still single. He was getting older by the day. There didn't seem to be anyone close to him bothered enough to persuade him to get married. For nearly twenty years, he had changed many jobs and apartments in this city. There was probably no Mumbai suburb he hadn't lived in and no streetside food cart he had not eaten from. For some time he had shared rooms with other bachelors who were not really his friends, but as he grew older, he got tired of living with strangers and took up quarters on his own. He used to wonder why he needed an entire room to himself when all he used it for was a bath in the morning and six hours of sleep at night. But when he realized that even with people he had known for years he could not share the sort of easy camaraderie that bus drivers had when they met momentarily at the station, he had given up that kind of living, and now for the last four years, he had occupied a small room by himself on the terrace of an old building. The room had a small square window. On the days that Satyajit did not go to work, he would observe the sunbeam coming through the window to make the room sparkle. It seemed to him like a broom of light that swept his mind, too. When clouds gathered, the rays disappeared. He always left the window open, even when he went out. On its inner ledge, his shaving set, toothpaste, brush, and comb shone in the golden light.

He often went to his colleagues' weddings, funerals, and other ceremonies. When someone tried to pull his leg about not being married, he would say, "I'm married to this city. Where's the space for another relationship?"

Since he lived on top of a three-story building, he felt as though below him lay an entire society. On the terrace was a silence quite alien to the people below, or to the noise of the road. It was as though he filled himself with this silence as he would secure his little room with a little lock and climb down the steps to go to work. When he returned in the evening and unlocked the door, standing in that same silence, it was as though the room had been waiting for him. In this room that no one else ever entered, only the sun's rays had come and gone, warming the space. A deep twilight pervaded the terrace, quite different from the darkness split by the lights from the bazaar below.

Today, like always, Satyajit woke late and rushed to get ready. As he was locking the door, he saw an old man

climbing up the stairs. Thinking he had made a mistake, Satyajit said, "There are no more floors here. This
is the terrace and there's no one here," making a sign
to him to stop. The old man tried to catch his breath,
and, hesitantly pulling out a piece of paper from his
pocket, said, "It's this very address. Satyajit Datta . . ."
Satyajit was irritated. He was already late for work. But
he felt bad about being impolite to this elderly man who
had clearly come looking for him from afar. "Come in,
come in," he said, unlocking the door and unfolding a
metal chair for him to sit on. Satyajit had never had a
guest in this house; the old man was the first. Looking
around at the small room, the man stammered again,
"Satyajit Datta . . ."

"Yes, that's me, Satyajit. I was just leaving for work.
Two more minutes and you would have missed me.
And all your effort would have been in vain. Tell me,
how can I help you?" he asked, pouring out a glass of
water from an earthen pot.

Drinking the water quickly, and wiping his mouth
with his sleeve, the old man said, "Perhaps if you're getting late, I should come another time."

"No, no, do tell me what you want," replied Satyajit,
trying to keep his shoes from getting on his unmade
bed as he sat on the floor.

"My name is Sanjeev Sen. Retired from the railways
ten years ago. I live in Borivali. I heard about you from a
friend who lives far away. I've come with a request. I've

brought a marriage proposal on behalf of my daughter. Her horoscope and other details are here," the old man said, proffering a brown envelope.

Satyajit was dumbstruck. It was like getting a gallantry award without going into battle. He pulled the sheet out of the envelope and glanced at it. Shalini Sen . . . education . . . date of birth, etc. The details had been typed on an old typewriter, and corrections had been made with a colored refill.

'She's working part-time in a travel agency. She's thirty-nine. Our bad luck that everything got delayed. We are willing to conduct the marriage at any time and place of your choice. If you want to meet her, we can arrange a meeting at a convenient place. Please give me your phone number. I will call you myself. I don't want you spending on the phone call." Looking around carefully at the small room, Sanjeev Sen stood up. "The address, phone number, are all there . . ." he said as he went down the stairs.

"Look here, I stopped thinking about marriage years ago. And I still haven't settled down properly. Perhaps I'm not the type to ever settle down. I'm a sort of wanderer. Look at this room. Marriage is not for me . . ." These words began to occur to Satyajit only later. This meeting with the old man had happened in a flash, and had already begun to seem like an illusion. Satyajit locked his door and slowly went to his office.

It was as though a new blank page had suddenly

appeared in his crowded diary, or a new pocket on the shirt he had flung on. It gave him a strange pleasure to think that the father of a "girl" had come looking for him—he who was past forty, graying, and leading an aimless life.

Satyajit did not have any friends with whom he could discuss this. What upset him was also the fact that this gentleman looking for a bridegroom had not asked him any questions. What did he do for a living, how did he live, what kind of thoughts did he have? How could the old man commit his daughter to a man about whom he showed no curiosity? Or was this family in such a terrible predicament that they were not interested in knowing such things? It began to distress Satyajit that the man had given him the daughter's horoscope as naturally as leaving a load of laundry to be ironed. Since the old man had been walking around under the fierce sun, the letters of the horoscope seemed to have evaporated in the heat.

Shalini, Shalini Sen, the name had some sparkle to it. She had been living on this earth the past thirty-nine years, and suddenly her existence and Satyajit's had come close to each other. Perhaps, he thought, she was the child of a migrant family that had come here seeking a livelihood, perhaps the family had never quite settled down. She would have learned to walk somewhere in this city, and grown up seeing lakhs of faces other than his. Speaking Bambaiyya Hindi, painting her nails in a girlfriend's house, dancing the garba during Navratri, going to the sea for the Ganesh immersion, shouting "Morya" and returning home soaking wet and swaying in the truck . . . This city had kept telling her "Everything will be all right" and then suddenly let go of her hand. She would have shuddered at that.

Left alone in the chawl, she continues to apply Vicco Turmeric cream on her face. She is despairing, angry, gets up in the middle of a meal and puts her slippers on to go outside. Avoiding her friends, telling them lies, she hides in a secret mirror. "You're so lovely, why aren't you married?" the loudspeakers from the marriage halls blare. Her face has suddenly aged, the hair at her parting turned gray. She has lost the right to sulk like a child. She daydreams about Pakya, who sells paper lanterns, or Kekoo, who runs the cassette shop. Slowly, like a book on the corner of the lower shelf, a book no one reaches out for, she has acquired her mother's posture and her mother's silence.

The loom of Satyajit's mind had silently woven its picture of Shalini. He felt a little weak at the thought that he had imagined her face to be dusky and beautiful. All his colleagues had taken loans and bought rooms of their own; acquired fridges, TVs, and mixers through installments; had wives who had jobs, and whom they took to the bus stop on their scooter, nodding at them slightly in lieu of saying goodbye—his colleagues who were diminishing slowly like a piece of fragrant soap in the dish in their bathrooms. But Satyajit alone had slipped to the corner of the world's eye like a sliver of bar soap drying in the sun; this fact was clear and un-contestable, like a bank account with a low balance. If someone asked him whether time stood still or was moving, he was capable of telling them clearly that he did not know. But now that membership in respect-able society was opening up for him in the shape of Shalini Sen, who was somewhere, breathing the same air as him, Satyajit found a new enthusiasm within him-self. During his lunch break, he dialed the Sens' care-of number.

"Who do you want?" asked a gruff voice. "No, can't call them now. I'll tell them to phone you. Is there a message?"

Before he could say anything, the person had dis-connected. Perhaps he had become a little too enthusi-astic, thought Satyajit, and buried himself in work. His mind quietened down as though an airplane's sound had receded into the distance.

That evening he decided to walk home from the station. On the way, he bought a tender coconut from the cart outside Johnson Park and stood there, sipping. The pickup point for the all-night luxury buses going to distant towns was close by. The buses started com-ing, swaying like wild elephants, to pick up passengers. The cleaners stood by the doors, calling out the name of the bus service and its destination. Satyajit saw a dirty little street boy, about ten or eleven years old, com-ing along the footpath, kicking an empty Pepsi can. He was making the can skim along without touching the ground. As he approached the bus stop, his can disappeared under a bus that had just pulled in. He stood waiting for the bus to move.

"Goa, Goa," bellowed the cleaner.

The little boy suddenly piped up and asked, "Cuddapah jaata hai kya?"

"No," laughed the cleaner. The bus moved away.

The boy picked up his can, but stood there as if he had discovered a new game. Another bus came by, with the cleaner shouting "Mangalore, Mangalore."

"Do you go to Cuddapah?" asked the boy.

Instead of saying no, the cleaner laughed mockingly and said, "Yes, we go to Cuddapah. Do you have money for your ticket?"

"No . . ." said the boy, looking away.

Then another bus came, and again the boy repeated his question. But this time it was the bus driver who replied, mocking him, "Here you're eating mud to survive, bachchoo. But what's there in your Cuddapah? A golden palace? Haan? In that Cuddapah of yours?"

Now all the passengers on the left side of the bus and all the people standing on the footpath began to stare at the boy.

Guilelessly he shouted, "Mera baap hai wahaan, my father's there," and walked away kicking his can. "So what if I'm a street child? Like you all, I too have a town, a father," he hollered. A shiver ran down Satyajit's back. Even if it was a lie, it aroused your pity. It seemed as if the boy had released his father from his obligations a long time ago. That can he was kicking along the street, his town that was somewhere on the map, his father who might be in that town, the moving crowds, the buses, the sex workers who got him to buy tea and bread for them and also fed him . . . all of these were part of the same universe.

In the dimming light, Satyajit climbed the stairs to his room and was unlocking the door when he looked around at the terrace and was startled. Leaning with his elbows against the parapet was Sanjeev Sen, who seemed to be looking at the vehicles on the road below. Hurriedly opening his door, Satyajit went up to the old man and found that he was drowsing. When Satyajit said "Namaste," Sanjeev Sen woke, saying, "Sorry, sorry."

"It's hot inside," said Satyajit. "Let's sit out here." He brought out a dhurrie and spread it on the terrace floor. Then he brought some water for his guest. The sun, which had left the suburbs, was still lingering at the edge of the distant hills.

"I heard you had phoned. That's why I came immediately. I would have come even if you hadn't phoned. There's been an uproar in my house ever since I met you. I told you everything, but I didn't mention an important fact about my daughter. I didn't tell you on purpose. Because if you weren't interested in this alliance,

then I would be spoiling her prospects by letting everything out. But there was a big fuss in my house about
my not having told you. Shalini stopped eating to pun-
ish me. That's why I've come. To tell you that she was
married once, for two days. Shalini didn't like the boy
or his family and came home on the third day. What
kind of marriage is a two-day marriage? And besides, it
was fifteen years ago. It has no meaning now. We live
in a different world today. But Shalini insisted that we
would be cheating you if we hid this fact. So I came."

Not knowing what to say, Satyajit tried to mumble
that Sen should have not taken the trouble. "But don't
close the matter now that you know about her past.
Do meet her once. Then you can decide. Please take as
much time as you'd like. But please agree to meet her."

Satyajit was beginning to get annoyed by the old
man's abjectness, but kept quiet for fear that he might
end up saying something offensive.

Taking out a small packet, Sanjeev Sen held it out to
Satyajit. "Please take this. It's homemade chutney powder. Since you live by yourself . . ."

Satyajit did not know what to do, because to accept
would be one kind of problem and not to accept, another. It seemed natural to take the packet, even as he
said, "I don't cook for myself. I eat out all the time, but
let me keep this."

Somehow emboldened by this, Sanjeev Sen said,
"Tomorrow I'll bring her to Satkar Hotel outside

Churchgate Station. It should be convenient for you also. I didn't bring any photos. Anyway, you'll see her for yourself." He stood up and leaned over the parapet again to look at the vehicles below.

Satyajit climbed down the stairs with him, intending to give him a cup of tea at the Irani restaurant and then send him on his way.

"You've just come back from work. Do eat something," said Sanjeev Sen, as though he were the host and not the guest.

Satyajit refused. In the long mirrors lining the walls of the restaurant, half a dozen Satyajits and Sanjeev Sens loomed. Outside, the traffic sped past.

Putting on a reassuring look, Sanjeev Sen said, "Only two days. In no way was it a marriage. What I mean is . . ."

Suspecting what the old man would say, Satyajit tried to look elsewhere.

"We have a medical certificate," said Sanjeev Sen. "It clearly says that her virginity is intact." These last words came in English. However much Satyajit tried to evade the man's gaze, there was no escaping that sentence. In all the mirrors, Sen was wiping his lips with his sleeve.

After Sen had gone toward the station, Satyajit did not return home, but walked around furiously in the narrow lanes of the suburb. He was aghast at the cruelty of a situation in which an old man had to speak to a complete stranger about the proof of virginity of his nearly forty-year-old daughter. Sen's trusting helplessness, the wrinkles under his white eyebrows appeared in front of Satyajit's eyes. Was it possible for Sanjeev Sen to utter that phrase only in English? It didn't seem to be the first time he had spoken those words. Having uttered them in front of many strangers, he seemed to have lost any sense of pain or humiliation and become quite impassive. It was as though this old creature was flinging the certificate in the face of those who asked for proof, calling them sons of bitches. The little Telugu boy kicking the Pepsi can and shouting in Hindi, "My father is in Cuddapah," and Sanjeev Sen establishing his daughter's virginity in English seemed alike in Satyajit's eyes.

This life in the marketplace—perhaps its nondescript familiarity compelled people to share private matters only with strangers. Or was it that this city did not treat anyone as a stranger? True. The lakhs of faces one saw every day seemed familiar even when seen for the first time. As though one knew the story behind each face.

Satyajit stood by the traffic signal. The neighborhood park was now dark. The Pepsi boy's footpath lay empty. A few women, wearing makeup and flashing nose rings, lingered by the signal, strolling toward the cars that stopped at the red light. When the cars sped off without noticing them, the women shouted, "Jao, jao!

Go to your biwi," and laughed, falling into each other's arms. The word *wife* sounded so different coming from them.

One of them came toward Satyajit, saying in Hindi, "Why are you running? Arre, at least tell me the time before you go." She caught his wrist and looked at the watch under the streetlight. "Oh, it's eight already," she said. Turning to the film posters on the nearby wall, and pointing to the face of Kajol, she asked Satyajit, laughing, "And is that your biwi?" before moving off to join her friends. They moved away to another set of traffic signals.

As Satyajit walked toward his home, Shalini Sen now seemed to merge with the word *wife*. Worn-out working women walking from the station were smoothing their ruffled hair, stopping to buy vegetables and biscuits, striding past Satyajit to get home on time. They seemed like hundreds of sets of clothes animated by one life. Each one of them walked as though under a spell. All those eyebrows, noses, sweating necks, tired backs, arms, the faded flowers—they appeared like different images of Shalini Sen. Like a river flowing unseen in a forest, Shalini seemed to be there that evening. These heroic mothers knitted sweaters for their children as they gazed at the abortion clinic posters in the train. Their images multiplied in the roadside shops selling cupboards with mirrors. In another suburb, in another set of shop mirrors, amid another throng like this, Sanjeev Sen—holding his daughter's virginity certificate—must also be walking along. Satyajit went to the nearby cinema and watched a late-night show.

Next day, waking early, he went down to the Irani café and made a phone call to Sanjeev Sen. When he said "I would like to meet Shalini today," Sen seemed at a loss, but then said, "By evening, yes, it should be possible. Six p.m. at Satkar near Churchgate."

On his way to the station, Satyajit saw the same people as yesterday rushing to catch the train, but this time bathed and perfumed. The mirrored cupboard shops had not yet opened. The saloon outside the station was open, and Satyajit went in to get a shave. For years now, Satyajit had stopped shaving himself in the bathroom, which had no mirror anyway. He did not need a mirror to finish his bath and comb his hair. Like him, in this city, the million faces rushing alongside him didn't seem to own mirrors either, as though they were beyond all that.

In this saloon with its wall-to-wall mirrors, a few people were ensconced in the revolving chairs, in various stages of being shaved or having their hair cut. These public mirrors, which included everyone in their reflection, seemed like the friendships among strangers bred in the city. They were all familiar with one another in the saloon, even if they didn't know one another. And far away, when yet another mirror shattered,

Shalini would walk out, followed by a sunbeam, walking from one public mirror to another.

That evening Satyajit reached Churchgate half an hour early and stood on the footpath opposite Satkar. The crowds pouring into the station glistened in the evening light. Satyajit waited until nearly seven p.m. without seeing the Sens, and then went into Satkar and ordered a cup of tea. Just then, he saw Sanjeev Sen struggling through the crowd.

Panting, he sat down opposite Satyajit and drank a glass of water even as he said, "Sorry, sorry, I'm late."

Satyajit called the waiter and asked for two glasses of lime juice.

Immediately, Sen said, "Just one will do. I don't want anything. I've come alone . . ."

It became clear that Shalini had not come, and Satyajit actually felt better.

"Forgive me, Satyajit babu, I put you to so much trouble. I prayed to God to give me courage to face you. Shalini hasn't come home since yesterday. Look at her rudeness . . . disappearing without telling anyone . . . And me roaming the city like a fool on her behalf . . . wasting the time of a respectable man like you . . ." Speaking with lips that had gone pale, the old man took Satyajit's hands in his. "We haven't slept all night. We waited all day for her to come back. I waited at home until five o'clock. If she had shown up, I would have slapped her hard and brought her along."

The juice arrived. Satyajit, not knowing what to say, just said, "Please drink." When Satyajit was about to pay the bill, Sanjeev Sen shook his head mutely, with the straw still in his mouth. How could he console this failed father, how to fill him with courage . . . Satyajit simply stared at the restaurant door. It was as though the missed opportunity had made the old man even older.

"Don't worry, everything will be all right," said Satyajit as he stood up to leave. Both of them walked out in silence. The crowds were still rushing into the station. Those who drank as they ran were throwing their empty Pepsi cans into a huge round rubbish bin. A posse of street kids would appear at any moment and surround the bin. "It's really crowded, come let me help you get on the train," offered Satyajit.

"No, I have some other work nearby . . . I'll go later," said Sen as he started walking away. Then suddenly he came back and held Satyajit's hand. "You mustn't refuse . . . please, don't refuse . . . Let me pay for the juice. Otherwise I'll go mad. Please, please—" He counted out thirty-six rupees and thrust the money into Satyajit's shirt pocket. "Please forget what happened today. If she comes back . . . one day, I'll definitely bring her to meet you. You mustn't refuse. And you mustn't tell anyone what happened today . . ." As Sen walked toward the subway, Satyajit saw that the windows of all the office buildings around them had turned red as they mirrored the sunset. Outside the movie house nearby, some men were raising an enormous billboard with ropes. Satyajit stood watching.

"Kannadi Illada Ooralli," 1999

UNFRAMED

GANGADHAR OF GOLDEN FRAME WORKS WAS BUSY WITH his annual ritual of removing all the objects in his shop and washing the floors with phenyl. He would dust and wipe the frames, the glass panes, and the sheets of plywood and put them back neatly in the shop. His assistant, Vicky, was throwing away all the rusted nails and filling the box with shiny new ones. The shop had been around since Gangadhar's father's time. Frames for women's embroidery, for actors and actresses, for Gandhi-Nehru, for school group photos, for couples from long ago who stood on either side of a plastic flowerpot with folded arms—this narrow shop, where there was always sawdust underfoot, existed to frame them all.

In his father's time there were only wooden frames. But now there was aluminum and plastic too, and colored frames and glass. Among the pictures hung up to attract the attention of passersby—pictures of landscapes, gods and goddesses, President Radhakrishnan, Tirupati Venkateshwara—hung the photograph of Gangadhar's father lit by a red zero-watt bulb burning like a small piece of coal. For them, it was as though one day, after years of framing and hanging pictures, he had suddenly stopped his work and climbed into the frame above.

Gangadhar began to hurry. He wanted all the frames and the glass sheets back in the shop before the sun rose higher in the sky. One by one, Vicky picked up all the framed pictures ready for delivery. Gangadhar separated them into lots and arranged them. The embroidery, "Welcome," button ducks, peacocks made from coins—these on one side; wedding photos in one pile; gods and goddesses in another; and individual portraits that had been blown up on yet another side. Gangadhar was always very careful about the last category. These portraits were usually of people over fifty, and were often brought to the shop by youngsters. Gangadhar could tell at one glance that these were mostly photos selected for framing after the person's death. Some would bring pictures cropped and enlarged from wedding photographs, or from other group pictures. These photos had a funereal look to them. Sometimes such pictures would be of very young boys and girls, or someone in National Cadet Corps uniform, and the parents who came to fetch them would have trembling hands when paying their bill.

When the cleaning was almost over, Vicky placed

before Gangadhar some pictures tied in cloth, and asked, "What should we do with these?" These were the pictures left undelivered every year. Perhaps customers got transferred, or forgot, or had money troubles. Most of the uncollected frames contained embroidery, landscapes, and gods, with a few being those of actors and actresses. As was his habit, Gangadhar started sticking slips on these saying "For Sale." Since these pictures cost just the price of the frame, people who had acquired a new kholi in a chawl, or moved up from a hutment to a chawl, often bought them. And this lessened Gangadhar's burden too.

But this year, as he was pasting the "For Sale" slips, Gangadhar sat up in shock. In the midst of these pictures were three portraits—a woman past fifty, an old man, and a middle-aged man. The three did not seem related to one another. Different people must have brought the photographs in at different times for framing. But those who brought them had not come back. And the pictures stayed here, like prisoners no one comes to visit. Gangadhar looked at them again. The woman's photo had been extensively touched up. A brush had been taken to the flowers in her hair, her bindi, the flowery prints on her sari. The two men's pictures seemed to have been blown up. Even though the pictures had been wrapped in paper all year long, the eyes hadn't closed, thought Gangadhar, feeling a strange fear. The woman's photo had an expensive frame. Then why hadn't the customer come back? Vicky laughed mischievously and asked, "Shall we put stickers on these, too?"

"Cheh, cheh," said Gangadhar somberly. Hesitantly, he looked up at his father's portrait. The ash from the incense had fallen here and there on the garland around the frame.

The entire afternoon Gangadhar worried about who might have left those pictures. Did they not feel the need to collect them, or had they also left this life behind, or did the urgency with which they had handed in the pictures diminish with time?

"Let's reuse the frames and the glass, and tear up the photos," said Vicky.

"Why are you in such a hurry?" asked Gangadhar. He would speak to Maayi when he went home that night, and ask her what to do. After his father died, Gangadhar would not take a step without consulting Maayi. Except for his father, everyone in the chawl and the locality, including her son, Gangadhar, called her Maayi. She was hardly ever at home, but this was not a new thing. Since Gangadhar's childhood, she'd spent more time outside the house than in. When Gangadhar was born, her milk was sufficient for a number of infants born at the same time in the hospital. It was said that even after she returned home, she would go regularly to the hospital to feed the babies whose mothers did not have enough milk. Gangadhar's father was irritated by what he saw as her crazy behavior.

Having fed so many infants, Maayi used to wonder how many of the young people she saw in the bazaar or the fair she had suckled. With Maayi usually looking after a boy in the neighborhood who had jaundice, or nursing some young girl with a fractured leg in plaster because there was no space in her house, Gangadhar never felt that he was an only child. He seemed to be part of a large undivided family. And the fame of Maayi's amritaballi decoction was another thing altogether. No one knew how and from where she managed to get hold of the herb. She used to dry punarnava and amritaballi and prepare a kashaaya. Everyone with a fever wanted Maayi's amritaballi decoction. Those who liked the taste would come up with any excuse, like a fake back pain, to be able to drink some kashaaya. Amid all this flurry, Gangadhar and his father were grateful to get a little of her attention and a morsel to eat. In later years, Maayi had developed another habit. She would go to the city's hospitals, seek out those who did not have any friends or family, and feed them gruel. The city's loom, which wove lakhs of helpless breaths, came as a boon to Maayi. Whenever she had some free time, she would carry gruel and pickle to the municipal hospital wards. She did this even on the day after her husband died.

At night, Gangadhar brought up the topic of his abandoned photographs.

"You have lots of space in your shop to hang up all those useless pictures of fruits and flowers and gods. And you don't have any room for these three poor memories?" said Maayi. "If you don't want them in the shop, bring them home," she added.

When Gangadhar's father died, Maayi had virulently opposed the garlanding of his picture. All this framing business seemed to Maayi like part of the funeral rites. "Why put a frame around memories," she argued. But it was not that she was stubborn about it for long. One year after her husband died, she said, "Let's have one photo of his in the house. Is it enough just to keep him in our minds? Shouldn't we look at him from the outside too?"

Gangadhar thought he would display his abandoned portraits in the shop front. "Why should you think they're dead?" said Maayi. "Maybe they will come themselves to pick up the pictures."

The next day, Gangadhar wiped the portraits clean, changed the rusted nails, and hung them up among the samples. Surely someone among the millions of people who walked by would be drawn by them, surely there would be some relative who would see them. Maybe at least one of them would reach its proper home. Vicky did not like this idea.

"Why put dead people's pictures in the display?" he wanted to know.

Gangadhar answered with ease, "Why do you imagine they're dead? They might come in person to collect their picture." Vicky laughed.

Soon, these three people who hung there disregarding the dust, the heat, and the wind began to seem to Gangadhar like people he knew well. It also seemed as though there was some connection between those three—an old husband, a housewife, and her younger brother, perhaps. Gangadhar went on stringing these wires as he worked. Customers who came to order frames looked blankly at the three portraits. What feelings they must have invoked in them!

One man asked: "Are they your relatives? These pictures have been here for a long time, haven't they?"

"No, no," said Gangadhar vehemently. He wondered later why he had denied the suggestion with such force.

One day a friend of Vicky's, a young stage actor called Bandya, was standing around the shop, chatting. "Arre," said Bandya. "This photo is so large, so clear. One can see it from the balcony seats too. It would be first-class to have this on stage." And he went on: "The drama companies of this town need pictures like these. You know, when we have to show the dear departed parents in a social play? Can I have them?"

Since they had featured in his display for a long time now, Gangadhar didn't feel as strongly as before about them. "All right, let them find a new use," he said, agreeing to let Bandya take them. When Bandya offered to pay for them, he said: "No, no money. But only one condition—if someone comes looking for the pictures, you have to return them."

"Certainly," said Bandya cheerily, wrapping the portraits face-to-face in newspaper.

As he prepared to leave, Gangadhar felt odd, and called out: "One minute." And immediately he added, "Nothing. Carry on," and sat down quietly in the shop.

At night, he summoned up courage to tell Maayi what he had done.

"Son, what would have happened if they had remained in your shop is exactly what could happen on stage. There's no connection between those poor creatures and your frame business. Is yours the only shop in town? There are probably thousands. That means abandoned photos in every shop. Think how many there might be. If you all took an advance, this wouldn't happen at all," said Maayi, laughing strangely. It was a laugh that put paid to Gangadhar's curiosity about which stage the photos would appear on, or whose parents they would represent.

In his nightmare he saw thousands of photographs being burned in the city square. The housewife's touched-up sari, the veins on the old man's forehead—the fire did not affect them. Gangadhar sat up in fright, sweating. The light was still on. Maayi was putting dried pieces of amritaballi into a pot of boiling water on the stove.

The following day, communal riots broke out in some parts of the city. The leaders, having set two communities on each other, sat back on the sofas in their houses and watched appreciatively as the TV channel put up the numbers of those killed. Those who had homes locked themselves inside without going to work, and those who lived on the streets offered their bosoms up to the knives. When names were asked, they hesitated. The art of stabbing where one plunge took the gut out of a man was perfected. In the hospitals, barbers smelling of spirit waited to shave those who would be operated on. No one came to claim the bodies lying in the morgue, or the people suffering in the hospital beds. Because there, too, one had to provide a name, and an address, and thus reveal one's religion. Once again a bosom bared, once again a stabbing. Respectable citizens phoned each other to find out if all was well, while laborers on the footpath stayed under the sky with their eyes open, spending the night like ghosts. Laughter was banned on the streets. Looking someone in the eye was banned. Schools wore the silence of hospitals. Ambulances shrieked through the night streets, requesting relatives to take away the wounded since the wards were overflowing.

Stealthily the shops began to open again. Gangadhar did not know what to do. Outside the suburban train station there were pasted sheets showing the names of those admitted to the city hospitals. People were jostling to read them as though they were looking for their children's high school exam results. Who knows what they were looking for? Maayi, however, wandered from ward to ward with her flasks of gruel and kashaaya, not listening to anybody.

During this terrifying time of curfews, a boy came to Gangadhar's shop. "Namaskar, I need some help," he said.

Gangadhar asked him to sit down and listened to his request. He speculated that the boy had lost something or someone in the riot, but that turned out not be true. The boy's story was this: he was an orphan who had grown up in the city's armpits without a mother or a father. He had caught the pulse of the city, and shaped his life according to the clocktower's hands. Now he drove an autorickshaw. He had fallen in love with a beautiful girl. He would do anything for her. He wanted to marry her—had already bought a real gold mangalsutra. He had purchased a jhopdi with a running water tap in Subhash Nagar. The girl knew he had no family, but had told her parents that his father and mother were dead. If they learned he was an orphan, they would not agree to the marriage. So when her parents came to visit him in the jhopdi, he wanted to display the photos of an old man and woman. He was even prepared to keep the photos with him forever. Gangadhar was shocked. He didn't expect this turn of events. The boy seemed honest and helpless. "If you had come one week ago, your problem would have been solved. Cheh," said Gangadhar, wringing his hands. He asked Vicky about Bandya.

"How can you think you'll get those photos back?"

said Vicky. "Who knows which drama company they've gone to? Why don't you ask the owner of the frame shop on the western side of the station?"

Gangadhar took the boy and crossed the bridge to the west. "No, sir," said the owner. "We shouldn't get caught up in this kind of mess. Above all, there's a riot going on. A time of death. Lots of work for us. In the next two months, we'll have to make a lot of frames. So why get involved in this kind of lafda?"

Gangadhar regretted that he had given the photos to the drama company when they could have gone to as good a place as the young man's hut. "Don't worry, your marriage will definitely take place," he said to the young man.

"I'd look after the photos carefully. Our marriage will take place in front of the photos. We'd give them all due respect during the ceremonies," the boy said pleadingly. Gangadhar thought of another idea, and went looking for the photo studio on the upper floor of the market on the eastern side. The studio owner did not listen to Gangadhar's request.

"What if tomorrow the photo owners come and raise a fuss about loss of reputation?" he said reasonably.

"Look here, sir, we're using them for an auspicious ceremony. No one can object to that," cajoled Gangadhar, but the studio owner would not budge. Gangadhar returned to his shop with the young man. "Come back tomorrow," he said. "We'll think of something." The boy put out both his hands and shook Gangadhar's be-fore leaving. When he closed the shop before dusk to go home, the neighboring shop owners were reading aloud the news of the riot casualties from the evening newspaper.

When Gangadhar reached home, Maayi was filling gruel in two large flasks. She had put her kashaaya into a thermos flask. "I won't be coming back tonight. I'm going to J. J. Hospital. There's a young man there, the same age as you. Patient Number 2132. The nurse was saying he was admitted a week ago with thirteen stab wounds. He has three fractures, including one in his skull. After he bled in the street for two hours, someone brought him to hospital. He's lucky—they saved his life after a number of operations. But he's lost his mem-ory. Can't remember his name, his family, his age, his address—nothing. He's like a newborn infant. If I stroke his back and look into his eyes, it appears as though he's smiling," said Maayi, as she put a pair of Gangadhar's pajamas and a shirt into her bag. "If I hadn't been there today, they might have discharged him, saying there's no space for new admissions. Where will the child go in this tomblike city?"

Maayi continued: "If needy people come asking for clothes, don't hesitate. And don't give them torn clothes. See, there's your father's wedding coat. It's quite sturdy. Give that away too. It will come in handy against the cold. And my saris are here." Saying this, she went away.

Maayi did not come back that night. Gangadhar took out clothes to give away. As he pulled out his father's coat, he thought how all the clothes would acquire a new life. As he lay down to sleep, Patient Number 2132 appeared before his eyes.

Having lost his religion, address, age, name, and surname, and become a human infant, this 2132 is being fed by Maayi as he lies on the bed. Unprotestingly, he is swallowing the gruel in small gulps. At the corner of his mouth, a sliver of a smile is slipping out. He is wearing Gangadhar's blue shirt.

When would the sun rise, when would he open his shop, and when would the young man in need of photos appear? Gangadhar waited anxiously. In the morning, he put the bundle of clothes in the neighbor's house and strode rapidly to his shop. The boy was there, as if he had been there all night. Opening the door hastily, Gangadhar climbed upon a stool. He removed the garlands from his father's portrait, unhooked the picture, wrapped it in newspaper, and handed it to the young man.

As though he had found a hidden treasure, the boy stammered: "This is enough for me, sir. Anyone would understand that the mother is anyway there . . ." He shook Gangadhar's hand and sped away like an arrow.

"Amritaballi Kashaaya," 1993

OPERA HOUSE

INDRANIL FOUND A RATHER HEAVY BAG WHEN HE WAS DUSTing the seats after the last show at the Royal Opera House, which is just shouting distance from Chowpatty. As he did when such things happened, he left the broom on the floor and came running out with the bag. Usually, when someone left things behind in the theater, they would come to the box office or, if the gate was closed, to the chowkidar outside. But since it had been quite some time since the last show, the courtyard was empty.

There were so few vehicles on the road that one could look down the five roads radiating from the Opera House circle and see far into the distance. It was as though people had evacuated the city, propelled by a great fear. But the lamps on the empty streets threw their brilliant light around. As if cutting through this brightly lit silence, the sound of a local train could be heard from under Kennedy Bridge.

After standing outside the gate for some time, Indranil slowly opened the bag. There was a thermos flask nestling quietly there. It was warm to the touch. Something that had to reach someone in a hurry had lost its way—Indranil felt bad about this. There was no use standing around, though. So he went back to the office, put the bag down on a small carved plank that had been there since British times, and hurried to finish sweeping the upper stalls. The three men who had been sweeping the Balcony section, Family Box, and other areas of the auditorium had already spread their little bedrolls out on the balcony porch and were playing a round of rummy.

"Hurry up! Shall I deal you some cards too?" asked Bhalekar, clattering down the broad stairs. On hearing Indranil's news, he said: "These things only happen to you. Don't worry, they'll come for it."

"When they see the closed gate and the dark front entrance, they might go away. I'll wait outside for some time."

"You're looking for an excuse . . . All right, come and sleep soon. If you like, you can hang the bag on the gate," Bhalekar scolded Indranil as he began to pull the grille door of the main entrance shut. Indranil came into the courtyard and sat on the neck of the fountain's cement peacock, shouting to Bhalekar not to turn out the outside light.

This old building covered with sculptures had

already started a conversation with the night. Once, the Opera House was a theater for dance-dramas and plays, but it had become a cinema from the era of silent films. At first, Indranil used to be upset that the intricate décor of the theater, which looked like the upper floor of a palace, was drowned in darkness during the screenings. While cinemas usually had the balcony only on one side, here there was a balcony on all three sides, making the hall look grand and luxurious.

Mausam and *Balika Badhu* had seen silver jubilees during Indranil's time. He had seen the film stars Sanjeev Kumar and Sharmila Tagore on this decorated upper floor. When the screening began, along with the upper floor, the stars, too, were drowned in darkness. Even then Indranil had kept on staring at those seats in the dark. When the days of jubilees passed and it was a great feat to have a film run for at least fifty days, a kind of dullness filled the cinema. However much Indranil wielded the broom, the dust was never dispelled. The taps began to leak. The hundreds of hands waving notes and coins in the interval, screaming for popcorn, samosa, and batata vada as if at the share market, were not to be seen anymore, and the counters looked deserted.

When the triplet theaters in Andheri—Amber, Oscar, and Minor—shut down overnight and a huge shopping mall was built in their place, Indranil's colleagues found other jobs and melted away. Trivikraman of the box office, because he knew English, became the sales representative of an ointment company. One day he was seen on the footpath across from the Opera House, holding a small battery-operated megaphone, shouting: "Take a free sample! Get rid of colds and headaches!" and applying ointment to the foreheads and noses of passersby.

Seeing his former colleagues on the upper balcony, Trivikraman said through his megaphone: "Indranil! You with your lovely name shouldn't sink with this broken old theater. Come on out! Come Bandya, Bhalekar, Maganbhai, come out . . . let me start counting . . . ten . . . nine . . . eight . . ." He shouted like the police did in the movies, flushing out hidden terrorists. They all came down to see him. Bandya even went off with him. Not feeling brave enough, Indranil, Maganbhai, and Bhalekar remained where they were.

While the others slept on the balcony porch, Indranil used to sleep in the hollow behind the broad steps. Once a week he went to the Anantashram khanavali opposite Gaiwadi to eat a fish meal. During the day, he worked at Nimkar Art Studio painting signboards. He could make the Devanagari script look attractive by giving it a Bengali touch. The taxi drivers would come there too, to get something painted on their back windshields. At night, when the shows were over, Indranil would walk up and down the yellow-lit streets. The city seemed to him like a mother watching wakefully over all the children asleep on her lap.

He must have turned twenty-five some years ago, but if someone were to ask him suddenly how old he was, he could not remember. At midnight, after the last show, there didn't seem to be an age for anything. It was five or six years since water had spouted from this dry fountain. Perhaps the fountain had last worked on the hundredth day of *Amanush*. His favorite Bengali hero was Uttam Kumar—it was he who had acted in the Hindi *Amanush*, and he who had come for the centenary celebration. On that day they had lit little colored lights under the fountain. Like a soundless spider without any great expectations, Indranil wove his small world around the Opera House theater. The night streets, the local trains, the colorful curtains of the rooms of the naachwalis that one could see from Kennedy Bridge, the Anantashram rice-and-fish plate, the round aluminum boxes containing the film reels—these were the strands of his web. Indranil had had no reason to disturb the warmth of this web. Because of the theater, the entire locality was called Opera House, and Indranil had gotten used to the idea that the whole neighborhood was his home.

The thermos he had found in the bag under seat D-57 in the upper stall had piqued his interest. It didn't look like a new flask. The soft white of its cap had lost its sheen. It seemed to contain some liquid, all right. Would it be a good idea to see what it was? Would it spoil by tomorrow? Would it spoil if he opened the cap? Indranil felt he should keep the flask with him. He got off the cement peacock, squeezed into the building through the grille that Bhalekar had left partially open, and picked up the bag from the box office. This was definitely a flask on its way to a hospital. But why had a person bound for the hospital come to see a movie? Or was it someone snatching a couple of winks in the cinema because he didn't have anywhere else to go, and had to stay up all night in the hospital, and forgot the flask while leaving in a hurry? Indranil pulled the flask out of the bag. The body of the flask had a dark red design like the diamonds on playing cards. Before putting the flask back, Indranil peered into the bag and saw a small piece of paper. He fished it out and took it near the light. In badly written Devanagari script, it said: "Nandabai, B 12 Sonawala Building, Tardeo."

Tardeo wasn't far. And sleep was not anywhere near. If he walked fast in these empty night streets, it was barely a fifteen-minute walk. Deciding to deliver the flask, he took the torch from his pocket and was about to slip it into the bag when Maganbhai came clumping down the stairs, grabbed the flask, and said, "Let's take a sip in the name of the lucky inheritor," and rushed back up the steps.

"Hey, hey . . . stop!" Indranil ran after him. "Don't, boys. There's an address in there. Perhaps someone urgently needs it. Let me go and give it to them. Please, don't drink that." As he pleaded, Bhalekar removed the cap, tried to pour out the contents into the cup, and hit his head with his hand, cursing the flask. There was nothing inside it. Indranil felt as though it was the soft cool night that was being poured into the cup.

Bhalekar grumbled that their hopes had been dashed at that late hour. "Indoo, please, go and fetch us some tea in this flask," he pleaded. Obediently Indranil took the flask and stepped out of the Opera House building, which seemed as if carved from darkness and light. To his right, in the distance near the Roxy Cinema, he could see three food carts silently cooking away. At this time of night, they did not need to call out to customers. Those who were hungry came to them as if sleepwalking, and ate with tired eyes. Who knew where these carts went in the daytime? After midnight, they would rise up in the empty streets as if from nowhere. Those who slept on the footpath opposite the Opera House were already sweeping their usual spots and spreading out their bedding. Sapan, a man who slept near the electricity grid, called out: "Indoo, shall we go and get a single palti egg to eat?" Indranil signaled to him to indicate he was running an errand, and started walking briskly toward Kennedy Bridge. "And who's invited you today? Parveen Babi or Zeenat Aman?" cackled Sapan, laughing.

It was a relief that the flask turned out to be empty. For no reason at all, Indranil turned to look down from the bridge. The Opera House lay below, looking helpless, without a trace of Maganbhai and Bhalekar. In daylight, its tower appeared as though praying to the skies, but now they had melted into the darkness. From the colorful windows of the buildings by the side of Kennedy Bridge the sound of the sarangi and the anklets of the dancers could be heard. Last week some of those girls had come to the matinee show of *Haiwan*.

"What's this we hear, Indoo? Are they closing the theater? That's our plight too. Who wants this singing and dancing these days? There are now dance bars in every single lane of Mumbai, and that's where everyone goes. Now no one wants to hear the songs from *Pakeezah*, *Umrao Jaan*, and *Mughal-e-Azam*. Only those penniless old seths come here now," said the girls. "What a lousy film you're screening!" they had added.

The fair girl Saavli had said: "Come to our kothi for timepass." He was not sure why she was called Saavli, which meant "dark." During the day these girls sat outside cleaning raw rice or haggling over tomatoes on the footpath. Somehow "timepass" had stayed with Indranil. There was no connection between the time told by the clock at Victoria Terminus or the one in the Rajabai Tower, and this "timepass." Or with the channawala, with his little round basket piled high with peanuts, who roamed there all day, calling out, "Timepass . . . timepass . . . with eight annas, timepass." In his basket, he even had a small firepot in which red coals shone through the holes. The channawala took care to keep the pot

warm, and moved it up and down on his peanuts, preparing his wares for his customers' timepass. Before, he
used to be at the Opera House even during the interval
of the last show. But he hadn't been seen lately.

Indranil always remembered the man's tiny firepot.
It raised in him the same strange warmth as the stove
his mother used to light during his childhood. Her face
would glow with the coals, calm, as though she had
just woken up from sleep. Indranil forgot himself when
he saw burning coals. In the morning, when Laundry
Babban poured coal into his iron and coaxed it to a
blaze, Indranil was usually fascinated. He helped Babban
fan the blaze. That heat, that forgetting of self, that was
the real timepass. Then what was this cold empty flask
telling him tonight?

As though the flask were leading him, Indranil descended the steps of Kennedy Bridge and stopped by the
roadside tea vendor. He watched him boil tea on a blue
gas flame and strain it before pouring it into the flask.
The scent of the tea seemed to blend with the yellow
streetlight and burnish the night. And the tea vendor
was like a mother stroking the night's back as it slept.
Picking up the flask, Indranil began to walk quickly on
the lower street to avoid being seen by the mischievous
girls of the kothi. As he went along, looking up again
and again at the colorful windows on the upper floors, he
heard a triumphant female voice saying "Caught him!"

Saavli and her friends were blocking his way. With

them was their well-muscled bodyguard, who kept an eye on them lest they be carried away by cars with black windows. He came with them to the pictures, too. Pretending to point a revolver at Indranil's chest, Saavli said, "Hands up! Hurry up. Are you trying to smuggle tea out of our ilaaka in the middle of the night? Hand it over." She grabbed the flask and ran into her building. The other girls ran behind her. "You can come too if you like," one of them called back. Helpless, smiling, Indranil followed them.

This building, too, seemed as old as the Opera House cinema. Dance-and-song rooms on the upper floors, a room on the right—where the steps began—where the girls lived. Without makeup and without Madam's clear instructions, no one was allowed to go upstairs. The girls sat scattered across their room, while one of them brought a few chipped cups. Saavli began to pour tea in each. As they took the first sip, a wave of good cheer spread through the group.

"Indoo, we had fried fish this afternoon. You do eat rawas, don't you? Will you have some?" asked one of the girls. Indranil declined.

"Why do you ask without meaning what you say— like Marathi people?" admonished another. "Just bring him some. Where does he eat home-cooked food?"

Saavli retorted, "Wah, my housewife, did your husband bring you fish? Hasn't your husband come home from work yet?"

"And you, my dear? What about your mother-in-law? So you can't eat until she's eaten, right?" snapped back the one who had been teased.

The long-faced Yasmin ran her fingers over Indranil's chin and said, "See, my husband has just arrived from Dubai."

Feeling tickled, Indranil bent his head and shook it. "Stop this nonsense of yours. Give me my flask."

Now Saavli got after him: "Hey, husband, didn't you bring me my cassette player and radio? Didn't you bring me China silk?"

Cute little Padmini said, "I don't want saris, I want foreign panties. Embroidered with flowers. When I'm dancing, I'll lift up my skirt—so—and flash the flowers!" She began raising her skirt as if in slow motion.

"Baap re!" yelled Indranil, as he snatched the flask and dashed outside.

The girls laughed in glee. Saavli shouted after him: "Fill up the flask again and tell the tea vendor it's on our account. Don't pay him . . ."

Obediently, Indranil had the flask filled. The tea vendor laughed. "Naughty girls! I'll take the money from them, don't worry."

In the cool breeze, Indranil clasped the warm flask to his chest and walked toward the Opera House.

From inside the flask, he began to hear the voices of Saavli and her friends. They played the game of house-house, of fake families. Their dialogues were all in the flask. The channawala's small burner, the chaiwala's blue flame, Babban's iron with the glowing coal inside—they, too, were in the flask. Bent on getting the tea to the silent Opera House, Indranil ran back, pushed open the gate, crossed the dry fountain with the cement peacock, and ran up the central stairs to the balcony.

But Maganbhai and Bhalekar had already finished their game and gone to sleep. Assuming they had fallen asleep just moments ago, Indranil said softly: "Are you fellows asleep? Hot, hot tea here . . . wake up . . . wake up!" But they were so deeply asleep that they would not have woken up even if all the bogies of a local train had gone over them.

Maganbhai's leg shivered in sleep. *Pity they slept without drinking this, and it'll all be spoiled by tomorrow*, thought Indranil, stretching out a hand to wake them, but then he pulled back. How tired they must be. Maganbhai worked like a donkey all day. All of last week, he had, in his spare time, gone through the cinema cleaning the fans and the colored glass chandeliers with his broom rigged onto a long pole. If any of them said to him, "Everyone who was watching the film is now back home and having fun. The film stars, too, have had their fun. Why are you struggling with all this? Stop work now," he would reply, "This is our home, fellows, if we don't look after it, who will? You think Amitabh Bachchan will come to polish this globe?" And biting his lip, Maganbhai continued polishing the glass globes of the chandeliers. Since he knew a little carpentry, he was always going around until the afternoon show began, holding nails and hammer, a saw, plastic fabric, and a large needle, repairing the torn seats. He had come up with the idea of stuffing scraps from the tailor's shop into the seats where the foam had gone missing.

Maganbhai and Bhalekar had been there long before Indranil had started working at the Opera House. They knew how to run the projector, too. Although they lay like fallen trees, and it would have been cruel to wake them, it would be even crueler to deny them their tea. "Chai, chai . . . hot, hot chai!" Indranil shouted. The two men sat up suddenly. Between sleep and wakefulness, smiling a little foolishly, afraid that they were late for work, they jumped up and started folding their bedding. "Hey, it's only two thirty. You can sleep for four more hours," said Indranil, and they sat down again. They sat quietly like obedient little boys as Indranil poured the tea into two glasses from the counter. As they drank the hot tea, they smacked their lips appreciatively and exclaimed how good it tasted. They lay down again, pulled their sheets over their bodies, and were asleep and snoring in less than two minutes.

Indranil went near the lamp and looked again at the slip of paper with the address. That address and this night were not connected in any way. The Opera House theater and this address were not connected in any way either. These sleeping men and the address were not connected in any way. Saavli and her friends and this address were not connected in any way. Perhaps the address would acquire meaning only in the daytime. When shops and banks raised their shutters, when people started moving about in their well-pressed clothes, the address would come to life. The person who opened the door would ask with raised eyebrows what the caller wanted. Would say thank you. All this in the daytime though. Now he couldn't take the flask anywhere. It had to stay here, like the spirit of the Opera House, speaking to the carved wooden ceilings, sewing the silver projection screen, cleaning the smudges left on Saavli's face by her eyeliner, blowing at the flame of the channawala's burner . . .

Having nodded off to sleep where he sat, Indranil woke with a start. A burning new day was prowling through the empty theater like an angry leopard. The other men were not to be seen. The empty flask sunbathed in a beam of light. Indranil picked it up and went into the foyer. There were a large number of people there. Maganbhai was gasping as he shouted loudly. It seemed as though he was weeping. Bhalekar came running up to Indranil saying, "Indoo, everything is gone. They're closing the Opera House from today. Everything's finished. Finished. Pack up your things. They've locked the gate. No, they're not building a shopping mall here. It's an old building, a heritage building, so

they can't touch it. Where do we go? Where do we go?"
he embraced Indranil as he sobbed.

Indranil was startled to think this situation wasn't
affecting him at all. In the bright sunlight, everyone
looked old. The peacock at the fountain was missing the
glass marble that was its eye. The posters of the film that
was showing until yesterday seemed suddenly happy
and liberated. Two policemen stood outside the locked
gate, rubbing tobacco into their palms.

"Indoo, go and get some hot tea. Let's drink to our
destruction!" shouted Maganbhai.

Indranil walked toward the small gate next to the
curving metal staircase, told Bhalekar that he would be
back soon, and stepped out. He had no trouble finding
the address in the daytime. Sonawala Building was opposite the twin Ganga-Jamuna theaters, and the door
of B 12 stood open. In the ten square feet of that apartment was a cot, a small teapot, a sewing machine in
the corner, two metal chairs, one folded easy chair, a
cupboard, a kitchen counter, and, between two drums,
an old woman with white hair who was cleaning rice.

Seeing Indranil, she stood up. "Come, come, aren't
you Anand? I saw you when you were just a little boy.
Come, sit down. Why did you bring the flask? Is your
mother still angry with me? Do sit down, you'll understand everything, I'm sure you will. My husband—
you used to call him Daya Kaka—he fell ill and was in
the hospital for a very long time. We had a hard time,

just like now. Because I had to take milk and gruel to the hospital and didn't have a thermos, your mother—Kundatai—gave me this one. My bad luck. Daya Kaka never came back from the hospital. They brought him home in the ambulance, showed me his face, and took him away. What could I do alone? I should have returned your thermos, but didn't. If the flask was sent from a house of mourning, I thought your mother might not accept it. I kept quiet, thinking Kundatai would understand. After that she came to visit me many times. But I couldn't bring myself to mention the flask. And then you moved away to Parel. And we lost contact. Much later someone told me that Kundatai was going around telling everyone that Nandabai had kept for herself the flask given to her in times of trouble. I felt really bad. I didn't know how to trace you. And suddenly yesterday I met Mr. Parulekar, who told me Kundatai was seriously ill and in Bhatia Hospital. I didn't know how to help or what I could do. This is another flask, not the one she gave me. This was left here by my sister. I begged a young fellow in the street to take the flask to Bhatia Hospital and give it to a woman named Kundatai Ghoghre, who had been admitted there. And that's all it was, Anand . . . I didn't mean ill. Why did you bring it back, my son? How is Kundatai?" The old woman began to sob quietly.

Having pasted handwritten posters all over the railings saying "All shows canceled from today," Maganbhai sat in tired silence. Seeing Indranil approaching with the flask, he shouted, "Hey, the chai is here!" Without noticing who was near him, Indranil handed the flask to Bhalekar and climbed the stairs to his stairwell corner, where there was a single beam of sunshine. The sun was cuddling the whole cinema hall, and this beam seemed to have come inside specially to console him. He stroked it softly with his fingers. The night that was hiding inside the Opera House rode out on the beam to mingle with the daylight.

"Opera House," 2004

A SPARE PAIR OF LEGS

JUST A FEW FEET AWAY FROM THE CROSSROADS IN FARMA-gudi village in Goa, six-year-old Chandu was jumping up and down, shouting "Mumbai, Mumbai," while his father, Narasimha, and his mother, Meera, packed a bag in silence. Tiring of Chandu's mischief and the hundreds of complaints about him across field and town, Narasimha had been left with no option but to take the boy to a remand home in Mumbai. Even the threats of the schoolmaster and the village police had had no effect on the boy.

It was already several months since they had written to Katkar Kaka, who had been living in Mumbai for many years, and got the address of the remand home from him. Even after beating Chandu severely, the parents looked at his small body, thin arms and legs, every night while he slept and were filled with affection for the child. In the dark, the husband and wife would

whisper to each other that Chandu would become better behaved as he grew older. But with each new day,
Chandu leaped to new heights of mischief. Beating up
his classmates was the least of it. There was the time
when he jumped out of the mango tree on top of Seetha
Teacher and rubbed her face with raw mango sap; or
when he mixed up the small change of all the flower
sellers in front of the temple and heaped it up in a corner, thus setting up a fight among them; or when he
shoved the pilgrims dressed in trousers and shirts who
were standing with folded hands just outside the inner
sanctum so that they fell into the sacred spot and cracked
their heads, still clad in the clothes they were forbid-
den to wear inside; or pushed Savitrakka's infant into
a bucket of water and tried to hold it down—hundreds
of such terrorizing acts were Chandu's handiwork. The
townspeople called him Gabbar Singh, after the villain
in *Sholay*.

If they saw Chandu coming, the other children
would flee as though they had seen a tiger. If anyone
saw a child howling on the street, accompanied by a
mother shouting curses, they would immediately know
that Chandu had been at it again. Sometimes Chandu
would run all of a sudden, like an arrow released from a
bow, through the women who were picking stones out
of rice, or rolling out papad, or weaving coconut leaves
together, followed by the person who was chasing him.
Even when he was running at that speed, Chandu did

not forget to kick the heaps of rice or the wet papad dough, or hit the shaven heads of the widows or stick a finger in someone's eye. Every night at lamp-lighting time, Narasimha and Meera waited as though for their punishment. Like searching for a missing ox, they wandered through the town calling through strangers' yards, "Chandu . . . Chandu . . ."

Sometimes, Chandu would come in quietly whimpering like a wounded animal and go straight to bed. Even if he had been beaten, he took it in silence. When his mother applied coconut oil on his wounds, and cuddled him, saying, "Why do you behave so badly, little one? Why behave like a demon? You sweet little baby . . ." he hid himself in her bosom, sobbing. They tried not feeding him. They dragged him to the police station and got a policeman with a big mustache to shout at him. It was no use. During a wedding in Kesarkar's house, when the guests were eating their lunch, there was a huge commotion in the kitchen. Chandu had peed into the pot of saaru and was being beaten by the cook with a ladle. He ran out, stamping on all the banana leaves spread out to serve the food. Narasimha and Meera, who had come for the wedding feast, had to return home quietly without eating.

They felt the entire town was turning against them. "Kali has entered into the child—he is a demon. If you leave him as he is, there's no knowing what might happen," said the townsfolk. So Narasimha wrote to Katkar

Kaka: "It's become necessary to put Chandu in a re-mand home. I'm coming to Mumbai with him."

When Chandu came to know about going to Mumbai, without bothering to find out why, he began to jump with joy. He ran to the temple, to where a group of boys sitting in a row sold flowers to the devotees. Among them was Kunta Mangesha, called Kunta because he was lame, who sold bunches of hibiscus. The boys surrounded him, chanting, "Chandu is going to Mumbai." Kunta Mangesha was the beloved older brother of all the boys, adored for the way he waved his arms about as he told them stories. Chandu was especially fond of him. It was from him that Chandu had heard about the magical city of Mumbai. There were many versions of how Mangesha lost his legs. One version was that he had lost them as a soldier in battle. Another version was that he had lost them in Mumbai. That he fell in love with someone whose husband cut off his limbs was another story. Kunta Mangesha had tied black rubber sheets to his amputated limbs, and stood like the disfigured idol outside the temple, waving his arms about and calling out to the tourists. Pretending to run fast even as he stood in one place, he pumped his arms and amused the children. And although the entire town hated Chandu, Kunta Mangesha always greeted him with pleasure.

On festival days if Meera prepared any special food, she sent some for Mangesha. If he met Narasimha,

Kunta Mangesha always said, "Your Chandu is a little terror. Very brave. Fit to join the army." Wherever there was a village fair, in Mangeshi, Madkai, Ramanathi, or Shantadurga, Kunta was there. Chandu wondered how the lame man got to these places. One day he had seen Kunta being lifted out of a bus at the Ponda bus stand. Once on the ground, Kunta crawled to the soda shop and drank a lime soda. On harvest festival days, trucks and tempos went through the town, displaying tableaux of various scenes and masked men in fancy dress. Kunta would be on a truck too, being the Appu Raja who couldn't walk, grabbing the band's bugle to play "Raja re Raja." On rainy days, he tied plastic bags to his stumps.

One night Narasimha said to Chandu, "Don't jump around with that Mangesha—if you keep on making mischief, someone will cut off your legs too."

The schoolmasters, who used to complain that Chandu was not attending classes, had reached a state where they wanted him to stay away. When Mangesha heard that Chandu was going to Mumbai, he began to sing the Hindi film ditty "Yeh Hai Bombay Meri Jaan," cackling, "I have thousands of wives in Mumbai."

The night before the journey, neither Narasimha nor Meera could sleep. Meera leaned against the wall with Chandu in her arms. Both parents worried that Chandu would get beaten up in the remand home.

"Anyway, Katkar Kaka is there. Let's put him in the

home for a few days. Then we can bring him back," said Meera.

"No, no," said Narasimha, swallowing. "We must be strong. This is all for him, or else he'll become a complete rogue. Let him learn a little discipline. Let's be strong . . ."

"Poor child, he won't eat a single morsel unless he has his piece of fish," wept Meera, kissing her son's arms and legs.

She went as far as the Farmagudi crossroads to see them off. The temple's flower-selling boys had walked beind Chandu as though they were in a victory procession. Kunta Mangesha smiled and called out to Chandu. Meera asked her son to fall at Kunta's feet. Feeling shy, Chandu bowed and joined his palms together in front of Kunta, who stroked his head and said, "You get very fine legs in Mumbai. You must bring me a pair. If you get a colored pair, that would be even better."

Throughout the bus journey, Chandu could only think about the colored legs Mangesha had mentioned. Were they really available? Mangesha always spoke the truth, so maybe they were. So Chandu would definitely get a pair for him. As the bus approached Mumbai before dawn, Narasimha sat up straight. Chandu, who had been sleeping on his father's lap, also sat up. By either side of the road, thousands of men had squatted like children for their ablutions. It was more frightening than disgusting. Trucks stood around, heavily laden with bags. At Dadar terminus, Katkar Kaka was waiting to receive them. Carrying their luggage, they walked a long distance to Kaka's kholi, which was in an old railway chawl in Parel.

"Chandu, my boy, why do you harass your parents so much?" Kaka asked gruffly, but Chandu was lost in gazing at the city's sights. In that old part of Mumbai, bankrupt textile mills were everywhere, looking like ruined fortresses. The blackened and cold chimneys seemed like hands raised up to the sky, crying. In Kaka's one-room home, Narasimha looked here and there to see where he could put down his luggage.

Katkar Kaka's wife was not around. Narasimha suspected that she had gone to her mother's house so as not to inconvenience the guests. More than three would certainly be a crowd in this kholi. Kaka made tea for them, and heated water in a large aluminum vessel for their baths. In the adjoining mori, Chandu splashed about like a sparrow. On the mirror hanging on the wall were a bunch of sticker bindis. Chandu couldn't tell whether Kaka had children or not, since there were no small clothes hanging anywhere. Katkar Kaka went downstairs and bought some bread for them. "I'll go to my office and come back early. Don't wait for me to eat dinner," he said, and left.

Suddenly Narasimha and Chandu were left all alone. Narasimha lay down and tried to nap, while Chandu stood in the doorway, looking out. All the kholis had a small veranda in front, enclosed by an old-fashioned wooden grille. Each veranda had, in a small used tin of palm oil, a tulsi plant, and perhaps a money plant in a bottle. Women sat in front of their kholis, combing their hair or cleaning rice. Men were setting out to work, holding small tiffin boxes. Children in uniforms of different colors were heading for school with their backpacks. It seemed as though the kholis were places where people came only to change their clothes. And even in that tightly packed neighborhood with those people walking so close to one another, no one seemed to have the time to look at these newcomers. The woman in the next kholi threw the fallen hair she had wound around her finger while combing it to one side. The ball of hair shuffled a little in the breeze, fell from the fence onto the veranda, and came to a halt in front of Chandu. Chandu looked at the woman and laughed. She did not even smile back, but just blinked at him and went back into her nest.

Narasimha went out and brought batata vada and biscuits for them to eat. "There's a hotel down there," he said. "We'll go there for lunch." They spread out the paper packets on the bed and ate straight from them. Afterward, they stood at the main entrance of the chawl and looked at the bustling market outside, which had suddenly come to life. The Parel railway station, from which hordes of people erupted when a train came in, was close by. Blind men wearing dark glasses stood selling lottery tickets. In front of a little shop that was closed, hundreds of small boys were picking up bundles of newspapers and then melting into the crowds. A man sitting on a little wooden box was counting out the papers. The small boys, talking to the man like adults doing business, would then pick up their bundles and go off. No one wore any footwear. In a few seconds, the papers were gone and the man's wooden box nestled in a corner. Soon a vegetable seller spread out his wares in the same spot. A boy clinking a coin against his kettle came shouting, "Chai!" Holding a tower of glasses in one hand, the boy pulled them out one by one to fill them with tea. Narasimha looked at Chandu meaningfully, as if to say this is what happens to children who don't go to school. But Chandu was already enchanted by the smartness of the tea boy and the talisman on a black thread around his neck.

Unexpectedly, Katkar Kaka came home in the afternoon, saying, "I applied for half a day's leave. We'll go wherever you want to go."

Narasimha felt rushed, as though he had to set off on an expedition even before he had recovered from the night's journey.

"You go and have your lunch," said Katkar. "After that we can go to the remand home in Dongri. No guarantee that I'll get leave tomorrow." There was no mention of Katkar's wife and children. He didn't ask after Meera. Neither did he speak a word to Chandu. Narasimha felt fearful.

"Come and have lunch with us," he said to Katkar.

"No, no, you go. Bring me a masala dosa," Katkar replied.

Narasimha and Chandu went out, looking into the kholis along the way. In some kholis, there appeared to be small workshops. Serious-looking young women were attaching something to pieces of plastic. Tiny machines were whirring. The women, whose eyes didn't blink, looked like statues.

When they looked back from the road, the chawl seemed far away. There seemed to be many more such chawls in the distance, as though the buildings had merged into one another. Hanging from the rusted windows were drying clothes, looking like faded flags on an old chariot. In the Udupi hotel, each of them ate a "rice plate" with gusto. When Chandu gently insisted on having an ice cream, Narasimha felt pleased, and bought him one, laughing. While Kaka's masala dosa was being packed, Chandu looked carefully around the hotel. The waiters were adults, but the cleaners were small boys, who dashed about at the speed of lighting. As soon as Chandu finished his ice cream, a cleaning boy picked up the plate, and with a wet cloth meticulously swept the rice grains from the table into his tub. Narasimha smiled at him and he smiled back. Chandu felt the boy was deliberately not looking at him. He saw the boy standing in a corner later, speaking in a serious way with the waiters.

When they returned to the chawl, Katkar Kaka had woken from his nap, and started gobbling up the dosa. Even as he chewed, he continued to speak. Picking up courage, Narasimha said, "Let's not take Chandu today. Let him sleep. We two will go by ourselves." Katkar seemed to be hesitating, and the reason became clear as they got ready to leave. Katkar Kaka started telling Chandu, "Don't touch this switch. Don't meddle with that switch. Don't open this cupboard." Then he peered into the doorway of the next kholi and told the woman, "Please keep an eye on this boy, he's a handful." Narasimha pointed to a packet of biscuits and told Chandu to eat some if he felt like it, and not to go out anywhere.

Chandu tried to fall asleep but couldn't. On the table in the corner was a square cloth bundle. It felt firm to Chandu's touch. It had been tied with two or three bedsheets, and knotted firmly. Chandu tackled the knot with his little fingers. It refused to yield. Breathing heavily, he attacked it again. Then suddenly in a heart-stopping voice, the neighbor, who came rushing in, shouted, "Hey, boy! What are you up to?"

After this initial question, she ignored Chandu altogether while she put two vessels she had been carrying on the gas stove and started cooking. Then she brought in a series of utensils, which all made their way onto the stove. After cooking for an hour and a half on Katkar's gas stove, the woman said, laughing, "See here, boy, don't tell him I used the gas, haan? Otherwise I'll tell him you were up to no good."

Chandu was frightened. Even though the bundle kept on enticing him, he stayed away from the knot. He went to stand on the veranda. The young women were hard at work on their bits of plastic. Just then, the tea boy came clattering up the stairs and began to hand glasses of tea to all the women, pouring from above so that there was foam on top. The women saw Chandu standing there, and signaled to him to come and drink some tea. As Chandu deliberated what to do, the tea boy came up to him and gave him a glass. The hot glass burned Chandu's hand, and he put it down suddenly, while the tea boy laughed. He was probably not much older than Chandu, and the women called out to him, "Popat, Popat, dance that 'hamma' dance for us!"

As though to indicate that he didn't have time for all this, Popat balanced a glass on his head, held his hand on his hip, and said, "Hamma, hamma," while wiggling his bottom. In a trice, he had moved on to the next chawl. Chandu laughed. He finished his tea and went over to leave the glass near the young women, who had already returned to their statue-like positions. The machines had started whirring again.

Chandu waited for Popat the tea boy to emerge from one of the chawls. He was back quickly, having collected all the empty glasses. As though he understood Chandu's fascination with him, he asked, "What's your name?" And when the boy replied, "Chandu," Popat immediately asked for the empty glass.

Chandu pointed to the young women at their machines. When he picked up the glasses and collected his money from the girls, Popat came past Chandu and said, "Maaf kiya, you're excused." It seemed as though the girls had forgotten to pay Popat for the extra glass of tea, but all the same he "forgave" Chandu, before he went back into the streets and melted into the heat, holding his kettle.

The breeze that blew from the side of the market felt hot on Chandu's face. He peered slowly into the neighbor's house. On a rather small cot, the woman, who was quite big, was fast asleep. A six-inch-wide electric fan in a small square box was making a "kiti-kiti" noise. Chandu glimpsed several cages inside the kholi, and wondered why rats needed such large traps. Suddenly Chandu realized with surprise that he hadn't so far seen a single animal—a cock, or a dog, a cat, or a squirrel. He began to think about Kunta Mangesha, who could cover his mouth with his hand and make animal and bird sounds. When he told them that yellow parrots used to come to Veling Hill, the children used to insist that parrots were green, and Mangesha would laugh and say they could have it that way if they wanted. Chandu wondered if this large woman was one of the thousand wives Mangesha had left behind in Mumbai. Then his attention turned to the mysterious bundle, and again he began to pull at the knot. Just then Narasimha and Katkar came back.

"Eh, eh, eh, don't touch that bundle," said Katkar Kaka, lying down on the bed. "Now you know the way to Dongri. Take Chandu tomorrow, and if you get lost, just ask a panwala." Then, uttering "My god!" Katkar shut his eyes.

Looking defeated, Narasimha turned to Chandu and asked him if he had eaten the biscuits. In a small voice, Chandu related the story of Popat giving him tea, hearing which Katkar Kaka, with his eyes still shut, began to babble: "You should never take what a stranger gives you. These street children are up to no good. Today it's tea, tomorrow something else . . ."

"Let's go and get something to eat," said Narasimha to Chandu.

"Why don't you go for a stroll and come back in a couple of hours?" suggested Katkar Kaka.

As soon as they were on the street, Narasimha hugged his son, and asked: "Shall we eat an ice cream?" Narasimha's limbs were shaking, and his heart thumping as if he had just woken from a bad dream. He hadn't recovered from Katkar's unexpected behavior when they went to see the remand home. They had changed buses twice, and then walked a long way to reach the home. Pointing out the rusted, jail-like building from a distance, Katkar said, "There's your son's remand home. You can go inside if you like, I'm not coming." Then

he burst out: "Look, Narasimha, I've done all this for
you because it's the first time you've come to Mumbai.
In the future, I won't be able to mind your rogue of a
son, or worry about his endless pranks. This place is
infamous for housing juvenile delinquents and homeless
children, and I don't want to have anything to do with
it. If you have the idea that I could be the local guardian
for your son, remove it from your mind at once." Narasimha couldn't understand why Katkar could not look
him in the eye. His mouth felt dry as he stared at the
remand home, which began to look like a graveyard.
In the heat of the afternoon, the building seemed to
be without human inhabitants. In that moment, Narasimha felt afraid that he had come so far from Chandu.

Father and son ate their ice cream. "Much better
than what you get in Ponda," said Chandu, smacking
his lips. They wandered for a bit through the bazaar.
Like in the morning, Chandu saw only children everywhere. Shoeshine boys, boys who scrubbed windshields
of cars with yellow cloths, those who sold rat poison,
those who held the ladder for the poster-stickers, those
who sold cilantro in bunches, those who shouted out
to customers from bhel puri and omelette carts—all of
them like himself. What brave children. Chandu felt
that all schoolteachers should come and see how these
boys behaved. Narasimha, on the other hand, could not
think of anything but Chandu's touch and his voice.
When Chandu said they should go and look at the trains,

they climbed the station stairs. From the bridge they could see Parel Station. Each train looked as though it was carrying limbs and trunks and heads from a far-off battlefield. Each would deposit some of these on the platform and proceed to its next destination.

Chandu thought he saw a familiar small figure waving to him from the corner of the bridge. He was afraid to look closely. But when he did, he saw the tea boy Popat, sitting on his kettle, his talisman winking in the evening sun. Narasimha took Chandu's hand and started climbing down the stairs. Chandu felt like a top that had begun to spin, thrilled to see Popat.

As they climbed down the stairs, they were shocked to see a middle-aged man lying on the steps and thrashing around as though he was having an epileptic fit. His body was arching like a bow, and his slippers and bag were scattered on the steps. People were walking past him. Some stood and looked. Some said he must be drunk. Others said, "Hold a chappal to his nose." One said, "Get some water." No one stayed beyond two or three minutes. But amid the crowd, speculation about who he might be continued. Narasimha sat down on the step and held the man so that he would not fall off. Someone took up the piece of paper the man had been clutching. When pulled, the paper tore into three pieces, and people began to scrutinize each of the pieces. The paper was torn from a school exercise book.

"There's some sort of map here," said one in a raised voice.

"There seems to be some mystery here."

"It's a map of some underground activity . . ." said some people.

"Why don't you join the three pieces together?" suggested one person.

This was done, and people peered at the paper again. "Perhaps it's the code of a smuggling gang," said someone.

"We should inform the police," said another.

Yet another man sat on the steps and smoothed out the pieces of paper. Immediately, Chandu figured out what it was, but did not have the courage to speak up. He whispered in his father's ear just one word: "Chappal." Then Narasimha, too, saw the diagram clearly, and began to tell everyone that it was the measurement of a small boy's foot, made to buy a chappal of the right size. The man who had been lying on the steps was coming back to consciousness, and he too nodded faintly. The crowd dispersed, feeling cheated. The man stood up slowly, and after they had made sure he had picked up his bag and had begun to cross the bridge, Narasimha and Chandu left the station. How quickly the boy had understood the diagram! Narasimha felt very happy. He held Chandu close to him as they walked on. "How did you figure out what it was?" he asked his son.

Chandu was filled with enthusiasm. "Appa, when do

we go to the shoe house Mangesha told us about, and the aquarium?" he asked.

"Tomorrow," said Narasimha.

They got back to Katkar's kholi a little earlier than expected. The door and windows, which were always open, were now shut from the inside. They could hear faint sounds from the kholi. Narasimha was astonished. He banged on the door, and the sounds stopped suddenly. Chandu stared at the door, which showed no signs of opening. Narasimha worried that thieves might have gotten inside. He banged on the door again. Then he climbed on the window ledge, slowly pushed aside the ventilator glass, and looked inside. Katkar Kaka was tying up something in the sheets with great haste. Suddenly Narasimha understood what the small square object was. It was a television set. Folding up the wires, Katkar tied the knots tightly. Having placed it on the corner table, he came nonchalantly to the door and opened it. Narasimha jumped down from the ledge. "Oh, you came back early," Katkar greeted them.

Chandu saw that the bundle had changed position and that the knot looked different. Katkar's behavior, like a child eating a tidbit in secret, alarmed Narasimha. Chandu touched the bundle when no one was looking. It was hot to the touch. That night as they were making awkward arrangements to go to sleep, a series of strange growling noises and the shrieking of animals emanated from the neighbor's house. Although it was a sound that

pierced the night, no one in the chawl seemed bothered by it. Noticing Narasimha and Chandu's stunned
silence, Katkar said, "Cats, cats."

Chandu wondered in fear where the cats had come
from, since he hadn't seen even a squirrel's tail that
morning. Katkar went on to explain that the neighboring woman's husband was in the business of catch-
ing cats and selling them to pharmaceutical companies
for research. The large cages he had glimpsed in the
morning rose up before Chandu's eyes. Katkar continued with his story. The cat catcher went around the city
with a bag and lurked about waiting for cats to come
by. He kept them in the cages and put them all into the
tempo sent by the company every morning. When the
chawl people complained, he had let some terrible cats
loose to frighten them. "Makes really good money,"
said Katkar, raising his eyebrows. The cats' screams did
not stop.

Neither father nor son could sleep. If Chandu had
not recognized the drawing of the child's foot today, the
poor epileptic man would have been turned over to the
police. Compared to these people with faces like torn
banknotes, whose main effort was to save their pockets
from being picked, little Chandu Gabbar Singh's pranks
in Farmagudi's fields and hills, alleys and attics, began
to seem like the god Krishna's games to Narasimha.
How scared the poor child must be feeling. Feeling the
boy's hot breath on him as he tried to sleep clutching his

father, Narasimha's chest felt a little less tight. He whispered in Chandu's ear: "Do you see how the naughty little boys are all on the streets without their fathers and mothers? You're a good boy. Tomorrow we'll go home, and you must stop all your mischief, haan?"

Chandu's eyes remained open. In front of him marched an entire army of brave boys. With baskets of roasted peanuts tied to their stomachs, looking like little pregnant women, they marched on. They would leap from the running trains so that not a single peanut fell. They held this entire city up on their thin hands, as though they were holding up Govardhan Hill itself. In their midst was Popat of the tin talisman, smiling.

All of a sudden, Chandu sat up. He had dreamed that the Zuari River in Farmagudi was swollen with rainwater. In it was a boat without oars, floating. Someone had put Kunta Mangesha into the boat, and he was drifting away, far away, waving his hand and smiling.

Seeing Chandu sit up, Narasimha said: "Sleep, sweet child. Tomorrow morning we'll look for the shoe house, and then catch the bus at night to go home."

"I want to buy the legs for Mangesha. If we don't get them, I'm not coming home," drawled Chandu.

"But, my child, I'm not sure we'll get them . . ."

"You don't know a thing. Ask Popat—he knows everything. He's my friend. We'll go with him," said Chandu stubbornly.

"Shh," said Katkar, turning on his side.

The neighbors' cats were howling. Chandu felt that Popat was standing outside that very moment, and stood up. He went onto the veranda and looked down. A shiver went through him. Down in the street, in the middle of the homeless people who slept on the road divider, Popat was standing. He was looking in Chandu's direction, the shimmering yellow streetlights at his back.

"Bannada Kaalu," 1995

INSIDE THE INNER ROOM

WHEN HIS WIFE DIDN'T OPEN THE DOOR, ANTARIKSH Kothari was bewildered. After standing outside his apartment door for half an hour, he'd climbed down the three flights of stairs and went into the street. Meera Kothari kept sitting on the sofa, even as her husband kept pressing the shrill doorbell. Finally, he got tired of pressing the bell and shrieked a loud "Hey!" When it seemed as though the neighbors would come out to investigate, Antariksh rapidly descended the stairs, clucking ruefully to himself.

Meera and Antariksh's household or conjugal relationship or whatever you choose to call it had now lasted fifteen years, and of late it had become so transparent as to be almost invisible to the eye—so much so that even they would wonder sometimes if one person lived in this house, or two. Meera was not even sure if

Antariksh, who had not come home in the last three, four days, was with his girlfriend Parul or not. Even if that were the case, Meera was not all that bothered by it. When Antariskh took off, saying "business," with his comb, some papers, and a worn calculator in his small leather case, and wandered from town to town, it was as if even he didn't know what sort of business it was. But he had never asked Meera for money. Neither did he seem to know much about Meera's own job in a small crumbling office in the Fort area. It was not clear whether it was a good thing or a bad thing that they didn't have children. But this was true: when they did meet, it was though they were meeting in someone else's house. Even when they sat opposite each other in their own flat, they spoke like people meeting at a bus stop.

Antariksh was obsessed by his "business," and Meera was crazy about breaking down the old furniture in the house and getting a carpenter to make new things— turning a table into a desk, a desk into a chair, creating cup holders in the chair's arms. In this house, which seemed to come straight out of P. C. Sorcar's magic shows, there was an enormous double bed that was its heart, its main support. Although the bed didn't look as though it was from the *Arabian Nights*, it was thick and soft, and all the household activities were carried out there: eating, shaving, sewing, nail cutting, etc.

This was why they subscribed to the *Times of India*. The sheets of the newspaper were spread out on the double bed. After a meal, the sheets were folded and put away. If Antariksh came home late one night and took up the paper, dry rice grains and tomato seeds would fall out. He would feel sorrow, wondering if any food had been saved for him. For the first few years, Meera would spread out the sheets so they could eat together. Then she began to reheat his food when he came, having eaten before him. After a few more years, he used to heat the food himself.

And now he eats the cold chapattis straight out of the fridge with the pieces of potato, standing like a thief in the light of the open fridge. He turns off the hissing radio. He then drinks down an entire bottle of water. Then he bathes, puts on a white pajama-kurta, turns out all the lights and fans, and goes to the bedroom. Lying asleep, huddled on the double bed, Meera looks like a creature becalmed. Sometimes she goes to the beauty parlor on an impulse and gets a haircut. On such days, Antariksh wonders which woman is lying on the bed, and is aroused.

When she put on a new nightgown, he felt the same way, as though he had found a new woman. On such occasions Meera would sit up in bed, and he would start babbling: "Today I went and saw a place in Malad. My friend wants to start computer classes, I can be his partner . . ." as his hands wandered over her body. But seeing her merciless eyes, he usually backed off and went to sleep. Once in a while when she felt like it, when she hadn't yet fallen asleep, she let him play with her like an infant. But after playing for a while, he would behave as though he had seen a schoolmaster, and quietly go to sleep. Later, they had separate pillows, separate coverlets. When the milkman or the newspaper boy came around, each would will the other to get up and open the door. Then the new day would take both of them out of the house, and the double bed stood alone and ghostly in the flat.

With such a routine, how did it matter if one of them didn't come home sometimes? Often when one of them returned and found the other missing, the person felt happy. Being alone was the great luxury. Sleep would be undisturbed, since the bed wasn't really large enough for both of them. No need to cook either. Sometimes while making small talk, Antariksh would say, "My wife bought me a shirt," "My wife has taken leave from work today," "My wife's phone call . . . ," etc.—but what image of the wife would appear in his mind? Meera had the same problem: "My husband has gone on tour," "My husband does business"—what husband was this and how was he related to her? Occasionally, when they phoned each other to say: "I've left the key in the dhobi shop downstairs" or, "I forgot to switch off the bathroom light," after uttering these words, the silence rang in their ears, and they rushed to put down the receiver, saying "Okay, I'm hanging up." Once they had passes to a film premiere given to them by a Sindhi friend. That day they met outside the theater half an hour before the screening, drank a cup of coffee, sat together and watched the film, and then went home together, but neither remembered who the person sitting in the next seat was. However, Antariksh had no time for such frightening thoughts. He was haunted by dreams of money. Where and how would money grow, how many times would it multiply—he drowned in such thoughts. To such an extent that when one of his friends introduced a man to him as an intellectual, he asked him how much money he earned.

Meera did not seem to be aware of how she had been slowly ripening. Now she ran the household like the headmistress of an old school. Her salary kept accumulating in the bank. When there was only one last hundred-rupee note in the cupboard, she would take out some money from her account. When her female office friends or the women she knew as fellow commuters on the local train invited her to birthdays and weddings, she dressed up in a good sari, bought matching bangles and earrings, and attended the event with enthusiasm. She would even get a facial in the beauty parlor. Coming back late at night, she would fling her sandals about, throw her handbag to one side, and fall onto the bed in her party sari, with a face like a paper mask. She would wake up in the night, pull off her sari, put on her nightgown, and continue her slumber. It was many months since the TV had broken down. It was impossible to get the repairman to come. When in the office someone said: "Wasn't that a fun show yesterday?" she would simply say, "Yes, yes," and smile. When she went through the clothes in her cupboard, sometimes their wedding photos would fall out. In the Ooty honeymoon photograph, she is wearing bellbottoms and sitting on a pony. After taking this picture, Antariksh had gone to a shop to buy a Nirodh condom and come back with something else because he was too shy to ask properly. Now all these memories had the faint smell of naphthalene balls. No Mysore Brindavan fountains gushed now. The mind felt tight, and she couldn't relax with anyone.

It was after a trip Antariksh made to Gujarat that something happened that should have been a blow for Meera but was not. After returning from this trip, he used to go out dressed very carefully, and suddenly one day he brought a woman home, saying: "Parul, this is my wife, Meera," and got them to shake hands. Parul was Meera's age, and was as plump as she was, with a pimply but smiling face. "Bhabhi, bhabhi," she cried, "sister," embracing Meera. Tomorrow was Antariksh's birthday, Parul had exclaimed, so why didn't they celebrate it here together? When Antariksh came back after seeing her off, it was night. Meera was waiting on the double bed with dinner: rice, dal, some papad. She spent a sleepless night, wondering why she did not feel envy, jealousy, or that she had been dealt a blow. Antariksh told her that Parul was a good woman, hadn't married, had been on the train when he was returning from Gujarat, that she had an apartment here in Borivali. For the first time in eight or nine years, they were celebrating Antariksh's birthday. Meera went to the beauty parlor that morning and got her hair cut and her face cleaned up. She bathed for hours, shaved her armpits, and wore a sleeveless dress. With her plump arms wobbling, she made gulab jamun. Parul came with a box full of patra, the steamed besan snack they so liked, and danced around.

It was not clear whether Antariskh's expression indicated pride or embarrassment. Cautiously, he began, in front of Meera, to pinch Parul, encircle her waist, or stroke her bottom. Parul, unused to a man's touch and no longer young, blossomed at every contact with Antariksh. Seeing this, and realizing that the reins were in his hands, he began to create an impact on her by doling out his touches. Meera was worried. She ought to burn. She ought to boil with envy. But how was it that she did not feel anything? Just then, Parul took a watch out of her bag and put it on Antariksh's wrist. As though at the peak of happiness, he pulled her onto his lap and bit her ear.

The three of them sat on the bed and ate. Parul left

after hugging both husband and wife. Having put her into a taxi, Antariksh bounded up the stairs. He and Meera spread the *Times of India* on the bed, cut some fruit, and ate it. Parul is a good girl, she must have spent at least four or five hundred rupees on the watch, said Antariksh, slowly lowering his head onto Meera's lap. As she was about to run her fingers through his hair like in a Hindi movie, she suddenly felt strange, and pushed his head aside. Then she turned onto her stomach and covered her face, lying down like a child with bottom facing upward. Antariksh sat up. Perhaps she was crying. He felt foolish when he realized that she wasn't. Feeling confused, he raised his hand to stroke her head, but it came into contact with every part of her except that. He began to enjoy this, but then she shook him off and turned heavily to one side. Antariksh went out of the bedroom and looked at his new watch again and again. Coming back inside, he crawled into the little space available on the bed and somehow went to sleep.

Next day in the office, Meera began to think of all this as never having happened. But Parul's perfume still lingered in her nostrils. Had Parul drawn Antariksh to her, or had Antariksh cast his net? So was Parul's waist smaller than hers? Was her bosom smaller? Or was love about something else altogether?

Now Parul appeared again and again in that double-bed house like a repetitive dream. When Antariksh

waited for his token at a bank, when he ate a paan outside the share market, when he hung on to a strap in
a local train, it seemed as though he was another man
altogether, as though Parul and Meera had nothing to
do with him. But if he stopped somewhere to urinate,
Parul or Meera came to pull the flush.

When he roamed in the bazaar with his leather
case shielding him from the sun, Meera would go to
a Parsi wedding and eat fish steamed in banana leaf. If
her new colleague, the young Kashmiri with a budding mustache, stared at her chest, she would pay him
no attention. If Parul phoned, she would listen with
interest. If Parul said, "Let's meet this evening and eat
pav bhaji," she would agree to go. Then by evening,
she wouldn't feel like going out, and go straight home
instead. When Parul phoned the next day and said in
her cajoling voice, "Why, Bhabhi, you didn't come.
You're a bad bhabhi!," she would say, "Sorry, sorry!"
Antariksh was not related to her, she felt. If he were,
she would be burning over the Parul business. Or was
she deluding herself? Unlikely. How many friends she
had in her office! Some said to her, "You're so lucky.
You're free like a bird!" When she heard this, Meera
felt like a large owl sitting on the frilled bedsheet of the
double bed.

When things were like this, it was not as though
Meera was angry about Antariksh not coming home for
three days. Then why did she not open the door? She

just didn't feel like opening it. Disregard or unhappiness or something else . . . After three quarters of an hour she opened the door and Antariksh wasn't there. She thought perhaps he had gone on a business trip again. Because there wasn't that much difference between his coming into the house and coming only up to the door. And besides, Parul had phoned that day.

"Where is Antu? Tomorrow is my hemorrhoid surgery and he knows that it's tomorrow," she had said. "Please, Bhabhi, do come," she had pleaded. When Meera was debating about going to the nursing home, Antariksh had come and pressed the doorbell and gone away. *Isn't he concerned even about Parul's operation?* grumbled Meera to herself.

Meanwhile, Antariksh Kothari had disappeared into the glimmer of Mumbai's night lights. The past three days he had got caught in some tiff with a Sindhi fellow in Dombivli. They had even ended up in the police station. After all the trouble, he had come home seeking sanctuary and that dreadful woman had not even opened the door. If it had been Parul, she would have run to open the door. Sitting on a stone bench, he remembered that Parul was going to have her operation for hemorrhoids. What hemorrhoids had she developed between her big buttocks? Shee shee—at least "heart operation" had a certain ring to it, but hemorrhoids? Parul would probably have to lie on her stomach. And the doctors would be peering into her, like into a TV screen? What sort of operation would they conduct? Antariksh burst out laughing. *Meera should also have had an operation like this*, he thought. Not wanting to waste his life in the streets of Mumbai, he decided to go and check on his business in Virar and not return for a week at least. Maybe then Parul and Meera would worry about him, he thought, striding toward the station. Once on the train, he fell into a deep sleep.

The next day, Meera went to the nursing home in Santacruz with a few pounds of fruit of different kinds. Parul was sitting up, looking pale and plump. The operation was to be that night.

"They've told me not to eat anything. For a whole week I can't eat anything. You eat the fruits, Bhabhi," Parul commanded.

Seeing that there was no one around, Meera said, "Don't worry, I'm here." She then stayed with Parul the whole time. She went home at night and put the fruit into the fridge. The fact that Antariksh didn't make an appearance even at the time of the operation filled her with surprise and even enthusiasm. One by one, she began to eat the fruit.

In the hospital, Parul swelled with love as she said to all the nurses, "That's my sister, that's my bhabhi." And there in Virar, Antariksh remembered Parul and Meera only when he got up to pee. Meera applied for one week's leave from her job. The following day she spent in the nursing home with Parul. Then she cleaned her flat, and put a new flowered bedspread on the double bed. The stale smell when she opened the fridge door reminded her of Antariksh's mouth, and that was the only time she remembered him. When Parul was released from hospital, Meera brought her to the flat in a taxi.

Now they both forgot Anatariksh with a vengeance and roamed around lovingly with each other. Meera made patra because Parul liked it. Every now and then Parul would embrace Meera. Meera felt a new spirit come into the house. Until now no other woman had ever lived in the apartment. So when she saw another nightie and other saris hanging on the balcony to dry, she felt a strange happiness. If Meera made tea one day, Parul would make it the next. As one of them took a bath, the other listened to the sound of the splashing water as she seasoned a dish in the kitchen. One of them held the fan to dry the other's wet hair. Meera began to bring Parul film magazines from her office library. Then they would discuss with great concern until late into the night whether Pooja Bedi wore a bra or not, why Dimple shouldn't marry Sunny, and whether Rekha was having a breakdown. When Meera was away at work, Parul ironed Meera's blouses, sewed on missing buttons. Some evenings the two would wear each other's clothes and step out. They would stop by the main gate and each would dust the extra talcum powder from the other's face. Check each other's sari pleats. Go to the beauty parlor together. Shave their armpits together. Laugh as though they felt tickled. Meera would pull out her old clothes and the sweaters knitted long ago. They sat on the double bed and kept on talking until late, and then yawned together. They would stand on the balcony together. Once Parul started sobbing uncontrollably.

Meera stroked her head and asked, "What happened? Did I do anything to upset you? Are you thinking of your family?"

"No," said Parul. "It hurts where I had the operation." Hearing that, the round and soft Meera stroked the round and soft Parul's back and comforted her.

Meanwhile, Antariksh had become tired of roaming like a gladiator through Virar, and decided to come home. He had found an old key for the flat in his Girgaum office. Catlike, he turned the key in the lock. The door opened. He switched on the light in the outer room. There was the smell of jasmine. He switched on the kitchen light. Everything was sparkling. There was a covered vessel on the stove. He raised the lid and found some oil left over after frying. *Arre, it looks like there's some cooking happening in this house.* Slowly, he came and stood at the bedroom door. A purple night-light was glowing. He was taken aback to see two people lying on the magic bed. He moved closer. Two sets of buttocks of identical shape, like enormous chickpea pods.

Both sound asleep. Throughout the room were scattered combs, petticoats, and magazines. He looked at the two of them. Something came up from deep within him and he began to make a sound like a whistle. At once, the two people sat up. Seeing Antariksh standing there like a ghost, they began to scream in their half-awake state: "Chor, chor, thief!"

Antariksh began to babble helplessly. Seeing the arm of one woman about to throw the alarm clock at him, he retreated to the outer room. He ran as though a huge creature with four hands, four legs, and four breasts was chasing him. Still hearing the high-pitched "Chor, chor, chor, chor!" he rushed out of the flat and descended the steps three and four at a time all the way to the street and then began to run. Inside the flat, the women still shrieked, and rushed around putting on all the lights. No human creature seemed to have stirred at their cry. All the other flats remained silent. When they peered from the balcony, even the leaves on the roadside plants were motionless.

"Parul, were you afraid? Don't worry, I'm here," said Meera. With shaking hands, she made hot tea for both of them. After ten minutes of quivering silence, Meera said, "If Antariksh had been here, he would at least have called the police. I'm leaving tomorrow. I'll go to my own home. You can die here for all I care." She began to cry so loudly that the double bed began to shake.

"But this is your own house, Bhabhi. Why should you go anywhere?" Parul wanted to say something like this but could not gather the courage. She kept wondering whether she should cry too.

"Antahpuradolage," 1992

DAGADU PARAB'S WEDDING HORSE

THE MARRIAGE PROCESSION TURNED FROM MULUND'S LAL
Bahadur Shastri Road toward the railway station,
wending its way through the main bazaar. Leading
the procession were the men of the brass band in their
glittering outfits, followed by the boys with their shiny
teenage mustaches. In the middle were the middle-aged
men in their tight T-shirts, bestowing proud glances on
their wives and on the bazaar shops. Next to them were
a bunch of dancing drunks, their faces smeared with
colored powder. Right at the end came the women's
group, like the brake van at the end of a train. Amid all
this, sitting on a starved-looking dark brown horse as
though he was welded to its spine, was the bridegroom.
The strings of jasmine flowers descending from his

gold-edged turban covered his face almost completely. The feather on the turban looked as if it were about to fall. No one in the procession could remember the face of Dagadu Parab, the bridegroom.

Walking a little ahead of the horse, like a master of ceremonies, was Balchandra Parab, the bridegroom's older brother, who had arranged for the horse to make the procession more attractive. He had gone to much trouble to hire the horse, and had supervised all the arrangements for the procession from their home to the bride's chawl. Now he walked ahead, looking now and then at the people thronging the bazaar and also at his younger brother on the horse. The look on his face seemed to communicate that this was the first time in their family's history that a wedding procession on a horse was taking place.

The procession was approaching the Shivaji statue. Just as they came near, an old motorbike in a garage nearby sputtered into life with a screech. This sky-shattering sound pierced through the bazaar, drawing everyone's attention. In a blink, the horse had run away, carrying the bridegroom with it.

One moment the horse had raised its front hooves and neighed. The bridegroom called out in a strange voice. It seemed as if he was trying to decide on which side of the horse to fall. As the horse vanished with the bridegroom, a cry went up. The people in the procession started diving into the nearby lanes in search of the bridegroom. Balchandra Parab tried to address the procession but his lips moved helplessly. He then rushed to the vegetable market. People were immersed in buying vegetables, in holding out their bags, handing over money. It seemed to make no difference to them that this horse had bolted. As though something had suddenly occurred to him, Balchandra rushed back to the street and returned to the Shivaji statue. He told the women and the remaining band members to stay where they were. The women moved to the side, since it was a busy street. But they ended up crowding the approach to a fruit seller's shop, and he chased them back into the street.

When this event was taking place, Balchandra's wife laughed out loud. She knew that her husband had deliberately got a horse for the procession to show up her family for not having done the same during their own wedding. Balchandra Parab was in a dilemma. "Dagadu . . . Dagadu . . ." he kept stammering as he went through the vegetable market and reached Goshala Road. The terrible question that confronted him was where he should search for the horse. And if he found it, would Dagadu still be on it? Or should he search for Dagadu instead? All the men from the procession who went in different directions kept looking at the side of the road to see if Dagadu had fallen down somewhere.

School students who had just been let off for the day swarmed into the street. Balchandra stopped some of them and asked if they had seen a horse going that way. He asked this question again when he saw people at a bus stop a little farther ahead, and was frustrated that he got no answer. And then he wondered: where was the fellow who was minding the horse? Perhaps he, too, had gone looking for the animal. After all, he would be the one most bothered about the loss. At that moment, Balchandra decided to look only for his brother, and jumping into an autorickshaw, he began to wander through the streets. "Stop here!," "Stop there!" he said from time to time. A pile of baskets in the distance looked like a horse. Someone on the roadside seemed like Dagadu. Finally, when the meter had climbed to sixteen rupees, he stopped the autorickshaw. He was by then quite far from Mulund.

Gulam, the boy who had brought the horse, had disappeared in the commotion. No sooner had the horse neighed and bolted than the youth ran to the station and jumped into a train bound for VT. The horse wasn't his. It belonged to Bhanumathi's father, Bhanumathi whom he loved in secret and lusted after in his fantasies. Gulam worked in a grocery store in Kalva, and while wrapping a package one day had set eyes on Bhanumathi, who lived in the stable-like house opposite. Her arms had attracted him. Watching her hang clothes out on the washing line with those arms turned the youth into her

slave. Her father was supposed to have once been a ton-
gawalla. Now he owned five tongas, and sent them to
Juhu Beach in the holiday season to offer rides for the
children.

In this house that seemed like a stable crammed
with tongas, horse dung, horses' tails, horse feed, young
Bhanumathi moved around like a swan, laughing and
then vanishing immediately. She, too, began to notice
the youth she had enslaved, and began to play with
him just through her glances. One day, the youth went
boldly up to her father and asked for her hand in marriage. In return, her father slapped him hard. Gulam
nearly died of humiliation. But he firmly believed in
the triumph of love as shown in Hindi films, and didn't
give up staring at Bhanumathi's white arms even as he
weighed and measured out grain. With a stubborn rage,
he began to cast his looks of love at her. He befriended
the tongawallas. If young girls came to his shop, he de-
tained them with sweet talk and tried thus to attract
Bhanumathi's attention. When his efforts increased,
she stopped looking at him. Not knowing whether he
felt angry or sad, he began to spend time in the Thane
tonga stand, gossiping with the drivers. During one of
these sessions, Balchandra Parab had come there to bargain for his brother's wedding horse. Gulam was filled
with a strange gallantry. "Give me whatever you can
afford. I'll bring the horse before dawn. But I won't be
able to decorate him or anything," he promised.

The next day before the sun rose, he unfastened a tonga horse from Bhanumathi's father's stable and walked with him all the way to Mulund to Parab's kholi. Those in the chawl who came up enthusiastically to decorate the horse were scared off by the animal's behavior. Without being able to do anything with the horse, they finally used a step stool to get the decorated bridegroom onto the animal.

In his fear of this creature, which seemed to have leaped out of the movies, Dagadu had almost forgotten his bridegroom status. Whenever the horse shook its head a little, he thought that he was finished. By the time the procession had started moving, Dagadu kept thinking that he shouldn't have been born as his elder brother's sibling. When the band began to play, the horse made a small jump, and Dagadu's bottom received a sound blow. He moved his buttocks to ease the pain, and received another blow in the same area, making him curse himself for having been born a man. The youth who was the horse's custodian walked along, indifferent to Dagadu's plight.

Gulam wanted to get away from the horse he had brought. But the pretty young girls in their oversized blouses kept coming up to apply perfume, and he couldn't tear himself away from the procession. Balchandra Parab had bought a Gold Spot for him as they were walking along. Just as he finished drinking it, the Shivaji statue incident took place and the horse bolted. Without looking at either side, the youth ran to the station, intending to take a train to VT and catch a movie. As he ran, he cursed Bhanumathi and her father and wished destruction upon them.

There in Kalva, Bhanumathi's father had woken at eight o'clock, and had danced with rage when he heard the news of the missing horse. He ordered his tongas to look through the neighborhood and see if they could find the creature. He filed a complaint at the police station. When they asked him what color the horse was, he couldn't remember and said "horse color." Meanwhile, Bhanumathi went in to bathe. As she scrubbed her limbs, she sang "Laalaalaaa" to herself. She was full of good spirit today.

Here in Mulund, Balchandra was hailed by someone as he walked tiredly in the heat.

"Arre, what are you doing here? I thought it was your brother's wedding today?"

Balchandra felt like beating the man up. For one second, he felt that the wedding mandap, or tent, the chawl, were all far, far away. If Dagadu and the horse were here, the wedding ceremony would have been over by now. Suddenly, he wondered whether Dagadu had indeed reached the mandap and they were all waiting for him. When he thought of going to the police station, he remembered the nets in which they could trap him for the licences he had not applied for—setting up the mandap, the loudspeakers, etc.,

etc. Dragging his feet, he slowly approached the mandap by two p.m. The women were drowsing in the heat. The band people and the loudspeaker men were going into the kitchen and coming out grinning. At three p.m., Balchandra stood up and addressed whoever was there: "It's all God's will. Whatever will happen, will happen," and ordered that lunch be served. The guests enjoyed the meal, hoping that the horse would not turn up to spoil their enjoyment. At his wife's insistence, he ate a jalebi. When he had to pay the band the entire day's hire fee for just the two tunes they had played, his heart came into his mouth. But he counted out the notes, making sure people were watching him do so. When the loudspeaker men asked if they should stay till evening, he shouted at them and asked them to leave. Then he sat down on a chair and dozed off.

Why had the horse behaved as it had near the Shivaji statue? The horse had been in the circus for a while. Then it had been part of a film set. The sound of the motorcycle gunning must have ignited old memories—who knows which ones—in the creature. It was at that sound that the horse had run. It was already angry with the early morning fuss, and this sound was the last straw. The horse galloped through the Rajaji vegetable market and within seconds it was on Zhaver Road, turning from there onto Goshala Road. Sitting

on the horse, Dagadu shook as though he were made
of thermocol. With what strength he had, he clutched
the horse's neck and closed his eyes to become one with
the horse's movement—Dagadu actually neighed in astonishment that he hadn't yet fallen off. On Goshala
Road, a bunch of schoolchildren shouted as he went
past. Dagadu's turban, however, fell off at this point.
The schoolchildren picked it up and ran after the horse
for a while. From Goshala Road, the horse went into
the vast St. Pais playing field, galloped through a herd
of cows, crossed two or three cricket pitches and a small
wall, slipped past a petrol station, and thus emerged
onto the Agra highway, running between enormous
vehicles, trucks and double-decker buses. From the
buses, passengers looked out at Dagadu. Now the horse
began to gallop. Dagadu gave up all connection to the
world, and flew along with the horse, feeling at one
with the beast. His job at the textile mill, his brother's
bullying, his bucktoothed bride-to-be, his tedious
daily routine—Dagadu felt he had kicked everything
away, and clutched the horse harder. At one moment
he felt as though he were Shivaji himself climbing up
to Raigad Fort. The horse was running energetically
on the highway, it galloped through the octroi post and
through several traffic signals, toward a goal known
only to itself.

After a long time, the horse turned off into the

bylanes of a suburb, and, snorting and breathing hard, came to a stop in what looked like a stable. Servants came out of the house and helped the drooping Dagadu climb down. They unbuttoned his gold thread buttons and put him on a rope bed to rest. He saw, with un-focused eyes, a girl bringing him a tumbler of water. As he drank the water noisily, she went off, singing "Laalaalaaa" softly. Without a word, in two minutes flat, Bhanumathi's father accepted this ready-made bridegroom as his son-in-law, this braveheart who had brought his horse back.

MANY MONTHS LATER, SOMEONE TOLD BALCHANDRA Parab that Dagadu was giving children rides on Juhu Beach in a large and beautiful tonga. That same day, Bal-chandra took his wife and children, changed one train and two buses, and reached Juhu Beach. On the beach, there were scores of people, scores of children getting rides in tongas and on camels, and balloons everywhere. Dagadu was not be seen. Balchandra walked around till his feet ached. He bought his children a packet of pea-nuts and made them sit down, and then walked around for some more time before he came back. Seeing his disappointment, his wife grumbled, "So you didn't find him? If we had, at least we could have asked him to pay for the wedding costs."

"No, no. That was the least I could do for him, being his brother," said Balchandra, looking helplessly at the sea.

"Dagadu Parabana Ashwamedha," 1987

GATEWAY

SINCE IT WAS A SUNDAY MORNING, THE FLORA FOUNTAIN area was deserted. On working days, the parking lots were full of vehicles and crowded with street vendors, but today the same space looked wide and bright and new. It was as though the bustling city had put on an undershirt and was sitting quietly by itself in a private domestic moment.

As she sent the children off to school, Sudhanshu's wife, Paali, had handed him a clean ironed shirt: "How can you sit at home at your age saying that you've lost your job? Go out and look for one. Find your old friends, and ask them if there's anything you can do." Her tired voice seemed to linger in the air. The two children, afraid to say anything to him as he sat dully, waved goodbye to their mother.

"Yes, sir, tell us about yourself."

"That's all very well. But what can you do for us?"

"Very well, but what's the guarantee that you'll work for us with the same ability as before?"

"These certificates are a quarter of a century old. Typed on typewriters that we can't see even in museums nowadays. Since your factory closed down, you've worked at nine different kinds of jobs in these ten years. Do you know what this shows? You don't stay on anywhere. You keep changing jobs desperately."

"Perhaps something's not right with you? How can we believe that you will stay with us?"

"Multifaceted talents. But what we need is . . ."

"This is all we can offer you at present."

"After we see what you're capable of, we can think of . . . Arre, you're leaving already? This is your problem. You haven't figured out what you want."

In these old Victorian buildings, in different offices, over and over again Sudhanshu had faced interviewers: one with glasses perched on his nose, another stirring a spoonful of sugar into his teacup, yet another ignoring the interviewee and speaking endlessly into his mobile phone about the fifth gear on his new car. Sometimes, seeing the tense postures of youngsters half his age waiting to be interviewed, Sudhanshu would sit there as though he were their guardian, and then simply walk away. When he gave his name at reception, the woman would always ask, "Where are you coming from?"

When he replied "Mira Road," she would laugh and say "I mean which company?" In that laugh of hers, and the look of young interviewers who lost interest in him after taking in his ordinary full-sleeved shirt, his trousers frayed at the edges, he saw an invisible despair. Where was the new world? When would it begin?

The men selling shirts, those selling balloons, and the calendar and diary men, had all been there on the footpath for the last twenty years.

But the fellow slowly opening his box and pulling out the key chains, I'm seeing him for the first time. He, too, looks like he's over forty. This nameless man with his graying eyebrows, who is past the time when he was a child in the cradle, when he used to be rubbed with oil and then bathed, who competed in school sports, lived different roles—now he finally stands here in Kala Ghoda, in two feet of space. How did he take the decision to sell key chains out of a small box? When he first called out—"Key chain, aapke naam ka key chain"—where was I?

Sudhanshu lifted his head slowly and looked at the Communication Tower in the distance. On this holiday, this thirty-story tower stood in silence like an enormous tomb. The two big antenna dishes on top of the tower appeared like begging bowls held out. Suddenly Sudhanshu felt as though his time was acquiring a new shape.

Sitting on his knees by the key-chain seller, he began

to observe the man. "Kyon saab, want a new key chain? Want your name on the old one?"

Sudhanshu said to him: "I want a key that will open the doors of good luck."

"And which movie is that dialogue from? Go become a dialogue writer, the doors will open for you," said the key-chain man. "Arre bhaiyya, you speak like an educated man. I'll ask you a question that you must answer."

"Yes," said Sudhanshu.

"See there, that's the Gateway of India—we don't know where that India is, maaro goli. But we can see that gateway up ahead. Now, tell me whether it's the gateway to Mumbai or the gateway to the sea?" Seeing that Sudhanshu had fallen deep in thought, the key-chain man said, "No hurry. Doesn't matter if you don't have an answer either. Don't worry. Here, have some cutting chai." Continuing, he said, "Where will you find a job at this age? Once our hair begins to gray, we become invisible. Come to this footpath. Sit here and sell something. Anything." He waved an arm along the length of the road.

By that time, a number of stalls had begun to open. Women with tired, sleepless faces adorned with makeup had begun to linger behind the pillars, waiting to catch the sailors from the ships anchored in the dockyard. One of the women came running to the key-chain man, bought a key ring for her small bunch of keys, and got him to put her name on it. "Asli naam, beta! Your real name, my child," the man kept on teasing her.

She turned toward Sudhanshu, tried gauging whether he was interested, and turned back to the key-chain man, saying laughingly as she disappeared, "He looks like he's on his last legs—penniless party!"

"The cage she's in doesn't have a lock, but look at her bunch of keys!" The key-chain man laughed.

The pillars behind which the woman had vanished had old Victorian lion sculptures on them, many with their snouts gaping. Hangers with nighties were hung on the sculptures, creating another stall.

Dear Time, tell me, when one could buy just about any-thing in this unfussy city, what could I sell to you? Look at my photograph of the school play. I was the postman. My classmate Chandrahas, who was the hero, is supposed to be somewhere here in Mumbai. The heroine Maya married into a faraway town, and died in childbirth. She used to have this photo, and so did Chandrahas. The photo studio in our town is long shut. Now a railway bridge runs over it. The train that goes to my town once a week from Victoria Terminus goes over that bridge. That town, thousands of miles away, seems to be connected to VT Station in Mum-bai. Even though trains disappear, and faces in the windows disappear, these tracks keep their grip on all the towns they pass through. So yes, will you buy this photograph? And I have all my certificates in this plastic bag. Whatever I could do with them in these forty-five years, I've already done.

They're frighteningly old, these pieces of paper. Once, I used to be proud of them, and they gave me inspiration, but now they're mocking me. They've held me back so that I can't see or do anything new. I feel as though clippings of my hair and nails are in this bag. I need to get free of them. Once I do that, I can do anything in this town, like the key-chain man. Without worrying about respect or humiliation, without arrogance, I can become light and new.

In a film, after the intermission, all kinds of things can happen. Lost children are found again. Villains beg for forgiveness. Brothers unite. The heroine's illness goes away. Or those who were found are lost again. Good men become badmaash. The hero dies atop a cliff. No, I don't want any of this. No shocks, no magic. Just an intermission will do. After that I can watch my own film. My Paali, who fell in love with me blindly, trusted me, who left all the conveniences of her life to be with me, now sits in our Mira Road kholi mending her old salwar kameezes from ten years ago and our old bedsheets. I want to learn some new skill that can make her world happy. Push me. My city, my nakedness, the morning that's given me my own shadow, lighten me so I can fly. So I can do what the key-chain man told me, and sell something on this street with dignity, without feeling any hesitation.

The unpeopled steps of Jehangir Art Gallery looked as though they were grinning at him. Paali's eyes kept on asking: "Why did you draw me into this? I don't know in what ill-omened hour I fell for your jokes. Now I've made a joke out of my entire life, haven't I?

"Aayi and Baba were watching TV when I crept away, wearing just my nightdress. For months, I hid my face, like a thief, from all the local trains going toward my suburb. You know all those movie ticket stubs I had saved from our outings together? They reminded me forcefully of something sweet. As long as you had your factory job, they did prompt me to think of sweet moments. The day the factory closed down, you came home drunk, with your hair awry. In that moment, the ticket stubs lost all their meaning. Under the bed, near the Lord's picture, in that steel box my tarnished mangalsutra, which would occasionally give me a fright when I saw it, still gave me a strange invisible strength.

"Stop being stubborn, Sudhanshu. I'll look for a job too. Our neighbor Shukla Bhabhi says she'll give me her new salwar kameez to wear to the interview. She says I look young only in a salwar kameez—otherwise I look like an old maushi bai.

"You only talk about your childhood. Now, what will you do about the childhood of our kids, flying past our eyes at this very moment? In a blink, the blue of the sky, reflected in the boys' eyes, shouldn't melt away, no?"

Memories of their children being born. Celebrating the moment when they covered their school notebooks with brown paper and wrote their names on top. The house was full of their books and their soiled uniforms.

Remembering when Putti had a stomachache on the day of her final exam and had cried even as she prayed to the gods before leaving the house; and Putta, the boy, when he turned six, it was as though he knew everything now and stopped asking for birthday presents. To which daily soap did these episodes belong? And the old scars on the knees of the children as they slept, looking more vulnerable and sweet in slumber—were they real or unreal?

Paali, with her hands between her legs like a little girl, sleeping without a sheet or a pillow. Before dawn, how she gets up bravely, lights the stove, and starts cooking breakfast. When the water comes through the pipes at midnight, she fills up a drum and washes three days' worth of clothes. What must be going through her mind then? She who came to my dwelling with just her nightdress? Paali, who made me stand outside while she pleated her synthetic sari with the gold border and got ready for the marriage registration? Have I pushed that sweet Paali from that moment of love into the pit of this daily domestic struggle? Where had her fearlessness come from? And at this same Gateway, we faced the ocean and life and everything. Now, eighteen years later, why does this same ocean look so different?

Getting ready to cross the road near the Regal Cinema, Sudhanshu saw someone walking rapidly across just a little ahead of him. He stopped suddenly. Paali! Having come from the Oval Maidan side and walking through this crowd of strangers, she was now going along the lane next to Leopold Café, straight toward the Gateway. He meant to call out to her, but his voice was stuck in his throat. For the first time he was seeing her without her knowledge, inhabiting her own moment. His Paali of eighteen years ago. Here is where they had walked hand in hand. And she was now walking in this same place, all by herself. Who was she? Walking in that piteous solitude? When he left that morning, wasn't she crouching down, stuffing their son's books into his schoolbag and making sure his shirt was tucked in? "Don't forget to phone Tiwari. We are the ones in need of a job. It's not enough just to call him once," she had said. How she walks in helpless thrall to this midday sun!

That faded yellow sari that he had seen only at home now appeared in this unfamiliar environment and her movements brought a hint of something beyond . . . *It makes some emotion well up in me . . . Paali, my sweet Paali . . . at this moment, how shall I reach you, how shall I console you . . .*

With a dispassionate step, Sudhanshu walked well behind Paali. As she neared the Gateway, Sudhanshu could see nothing but her. She stood there under the arch like a schoolgirl on a tour. What was she looking at with her head raised? The curls on her forehead danced in the sea breeze.

Putti's nose is like mine. Putta's eyes are like yours. His right elbow has a sweet little curve that looks like your right hand. This time that grew from us, grew out of us, what do you search for beyond that, Paali?

This city, these buildings, the pigeons, the key-chain man, the sea—don't you see them like I do? Like the small drops of sweat on our Putti's forehead. Like Putta standing naked in the bathroom waiting to be bathed. Like the fragrance on your synthetic wedding sari with its gold border sitting in the cupboard. Don't all of these appear the same to both of us? Isn't this world like our children? Won't this entire world fit inside our little ten-by-ten-foot kholi? What is there to be seen beyond this? Give me your strength, Paali. Is there a door to this gateway? And aren't our Putta and Putti moving about in their own space this very second? Isn't every living creature doing the same thing? Is the Gateway showing us how to live with the rest of the world?

A colorful launch that took passengers on a one-hour tour of the harbor rocked on the waves near the steps. Couples and families were buying tickets and climbing into the cruise boat. Taking their tickets, the cleaner was stretching out a hand and pulling each passenger into the boat. Paali went slowly down the steps, bought a ticket, and approached the launch. Grasping the outstretched hand and jumping into the boat, laughing slightly at her fear, Paali sat down on the bright blue seat. She was the only person who was by herself. She sat looking into the distance.

The launch pushed away from the Gateway pier and

began to move ahead, creating its own little waves. As he waited for its return, Sudhanshu began to look at the world with a child's eyes as though it had been created anew.

"Gateway," 2003

CRESCENT MOON

THE ROWS OF EMPTY DOUBLE-DECKER BUSES AND REGULAR buses lined up in the Ghatkopar Depot were oblivious to the small ruckus taking place in the control room. The driver Pandurang Khot was pleading and arguing tearfully with Sawant, his shift in-charge, to give him leave for the Ganesh Utsav holidays. Sawant was shaking his head firmly and adding ghee by the spoonful to stoke the fire of Pandurang's rage. For the last twenty years, Pandurang had gone, without fail, to his village near Ratnagiri to celebrate the festival. For Pandurang, the festival was the high point of the entire year: from bringing home the Ganesha idol, the daily worship, the offering of fruit, the aartis, the playing of ghumat drums, the singing of bhajans for five days, to the village play in which he acted a small role, and the immersion of the god in the river while getting wet in the occasional light shower. Besides, Desai Master had said this year he was going to get a big part in the play. For this, he had already bought a pair of white shoes, a leather belt, and dark glasses. He had also been informed that this year they were going to invite a guest artiste, a tamasha actress from the city. Pandurang had been instructed to bring a set of false whiskers for the person playing Valmiki. Having acquired all this, and dreaming of playing host to the tamasha artiste in his own house, Pandurang had been waiting for a week to go home, but was now looking at Sawant, who, like a mute but wicked god, simply stood there shaking his head, saying, "Nothing doing."

Having finished their shifts, the drivers and conductors were washing their lunch boxes under the tap in the corner and getting ready to leave for the day. They watched Pandurang with some amusement. The joke was that Sawant had just the previous year worked with Pandurang as his conductor and was now his boss and shift in-charge. Sawant was rubbing chuna and tobacco together in his palm, as if saying, "Are you the only one who wants leave? Doesn't everyone want to celebrate the festival? All these years you got away with it, now I'll see how you get your way."

Pandurang, who had a reputation for being a little stupid, never blabbed the details of his personal life to anyone. If he did, the entire depot would be roaring with laughter at his discomfiture. Everyone used to tease him about his habit of looking at himself in the mirror constantly and making faces, like an actor re-hearsing a part. Noticing his peculiar habit of choosing to work only the night shift, his colleagues used to say, "And who does the shift in your house?" And when his daughter was born, they mocked, "Arre, Pandu, how did this happen? While you were on the night shift?" Pandurang did not listen to them, absorbed in his night duty, his bus, his lunch box, his thoughts.

When Sawant, who used to work by his side, got his promotion, Pandurang experienced his pain all alone. But he was sure of one thing—Sawant would give him leave whenever he asked for it. That same Sawant had shared with Pandurang the issue of his wife Sarojini's greed for gold. Every month Sarojinibai would eat her husband's head, asking for a new gold ornament. At that time every month, Sawant would reach for a quarter bottle, pour himself a drink, pass some peanuts to Pandu, who did not touch alcohol, and drawl, "La-dies' problem, ladies' problem." Pandurang listened to him for hours, his silence providing a sort of comfort to Sawant. The next morning Sawant would ring the bell, "Trin, trin, trin," as Pandu gritted his teeth and clutched the steering wheel as he maneuvered the bus in reverse. For this same Sawant, Pandu used to bring a half pound of cashew nuts from his village.

Knowing all this, their other colleagues watched Sawant shaking his head at Pandu and were vastly amused. Pandu had had enough. He banged the door of the control room as he rushed out. It was eleven at night. A powerful yellow light was shining down on the depot. Alone, Pandu walked toward the silent rows of buses. Suddenly, he screamed and raised his hands to the skies under that yellow light as he danced in rage. He ran toward his beloved bus, MHE 4388, jumped in, started the engine, took the bus around the depot once, and then went through the main gate. Seeing the bus with no headlights on, the sentry at the gate laughed and said, "Pandu," as he made an entry in his register. *How quietly he went off on his shift with his tail between his legs*, thought Sawant, yawning. In the distance, on the Western Express Highway, rows and rows of vehicles were moving. Sawant couldn't see if Pandu's double-decker bus had joined the stream.

As the night wore on, the bus left its familiar roads and went far beyond the suburbs and their twinkling lights. Turning toward the hills of the Western Ghats, the bus began to rush along. As it left behind the smells of petrol, diesel, smoke, and factories and sped through green forests, a fresh breeze began to blow through the entire vehicle. Singing aloud songs from Bal Gandharva plays, Pandurang Khot drove with concentration toward his home in Ratnagiri. Through this new world filled with night butterflies, jewel bugs, glowworms, clouds that looked as though they were brushing against the waxing moon, glistening in the rain, the enormous double-decker bus without a conductor or passengers galloped happily. Vehicles bound for Mumbai stared in surprise and amusement at this bus that had run away from the city. Pandurang drove on in excitement and passion. Climbing down Mahad Ghat with some difficulty, Pandurang drove on resolutely without slackening his grip on the wheel, and by sunrise he was in Ratnagiri. Shining in the rays of the morning sun, the red double-decker bus arrived at the little green village as though its inhabitants had dreamed it up. Pandu jumped down from his vehicle like a messenger of god.

The whole village reverberated with the news that Pandu had arrived. His friends came running to see him. But Pandurang's wife, who had arrived a week earlier to help with the arrangements for the festival, felt afraid. Even as everyone was in high spirits, she asked her husband to come straight inside the house, and took him into an inner room. Pandu's little daughter felt as though the Mumbai of her terrible school had suddenly appeared in front of the village house. But even while the others stood around looking at the bus, she climbed up the metal staircase, walked about inside, stuck a hand outside the window, and began to call to her friends: "Shaloo, Neema . . ."

Coming out after his whispered conversation with his wife, Pandu saw that his bus had become a human mountain. As though they were off to a wedding, the villagers and their children had occupied the entire bus. "Pandu Maharaj ki jai!" they cheered. "Victory to

Emperor Pandu!" Pandu's feet did not remain on the ground. He climbed into the driver's seat as though into the cockpit of an airplane, and with great style drove the bus around the maidan. As the cheers became louder, Pandu felt a momentary pang, which he soon ignored. As he got off the bus, in front of him stood Kuwalekar, the president of the village dramatic society. He came closer and whispered in Pandu's ear, "We've brought an actress from Kolhapur. Jueebai. Hurry up and come to the rehearsal."

"Coming right away," said Pandu, dashing into his house to have a bath.

His wife ran after him. Pandurang's father came out on his faltering feet, and with a strange hauteur made the people move away from the bus. Then he climbed into the bus with his granddaughter's help and rang the conductor's bell once. Liking the sound, he rang it a few more times.

Hearing it in the bathroom, Pandu yelled, "Who's making that noise?"

By this time, Pandu's wife had prepared a story in which he had got "special permission" to bring the bus to help the village people during the Ganesh festival, or Chauthi. Soon, she even began to believe her own story. The house was filled with a new enthusiasm for the festival. But Pandurang's older brother was suspicious. He had worked in the transport office in the Mahad section, and had never heard of an incident like this one. This made him more than a little concerned. This enormous bus, sitting like an Airavata in their court-yard, should go. He warned his wife and children not to show so much enthusiasm, and they began to go around with pinched faces as though expecting a catastrophe to happen. This made Pandu's wife rush around eagerly. "They've told him he can keep it for as long as he likes," she bragged.

Their daughter clapped her hands, laughing as she jumped up and down. Eating breakfast after his bath, Pandu walked to the front yard of the village temple, where the rehearsals were being held. Before he left, he told all the members of his household to keep an eye on the bus. His father said, "Come home quickly. We have to bring the Ganesha idol home. Perhaps we can bring it on the bus." Pandu's wife clucked her tongue disapprovingly.

The news of Pandu's arrival had already reached the rehearsal. Desai Master came out to welcome him, saying that since there were only five days left before the performance, Pandu should come to the rehears-als regularly and learn the dialogues by heart. Pandu's eyes searched for the actress. Kuwalekar understood his anxiety and whispered, "She's in the next room. She'll come out only when her role is required."

In a few moments Jueebai appeared. Her pride in be-ing an actress from a prestigious tamasha troupe from Kolhapur seemed literally to weigh heavily around her exposed waist as she walked in. Pandu was floored by her demeanor. She had a sharp nose. There were rings of sleeplessness around her eyes. But the way she walked or stood was striking. "And who are all of you artistes?" she seemed to say dismissively. Once her two or three dialogues were over, she disappeared into her room. Kuwalekar went after her, signaling to Pandu to follow him. Not bothering to worry what Desai Master might think, Pandu went behind Kuwalekar shamelessly. In her room, Jueebai had taken off her sari pallu and was fanning herself with it, complaining of the heat. Even after the men came in, she continued to fan herself, to Pandu's titillated surprise. Kuwalekar introduced him, saying he had come especially from Mumbai for the play, and had even brought a double-decker bus with him.

"Wah, wah," said the actress, moving to the window to spit out the betel nut in her mouth.

As she moved around rapidly, what made Pandu distraught were the globes in her blouse, perfectly outlined as though drawn with compasses. *This marital life is a total waste*, thought Pandu sadly. As though she knew that Pandu could not tear his eyes away from her blouse, Jueebai continued to fan herself artfully. When Kuwalekar got up to leave, Pandu said to Jueebai, "Please come to our house. We have a Ganesha installed. Please have dinner with us tonight."

She said, "Certainly, certainly," looking into his eyes, and Pandu was rendered speechless.

By the time he came back home holding the script of his dialogues, the preparations to welcome Ganesha were in place. The children were sitting inside the bus, beating the dholak and sounding the cymbals. "The actress is coming to have dinner with us," Pandu said to everyone in his house. If she came around the time of the evening bhajan, he thought he could sing a song or two from an old play to impress her. He began to hum one under his breath.

After a late lunch, Pandu was trying to take a nap when his wife poked him gently in the ribs, saying, "Whatever got into you that you brought this bus here? I suppose you'll lose your job now . . ."

"Shut up!" he shouted at her. "You should have been that Sawant's wife. Would have served that bastard right."

"Then I would have got some jewelry every month, at least," she said huffily, and vanished.

Pandu couldn't sleep after that. He went out, climbed into the bus, climbed to the upper deck, and stretched out on the long seat at the back. Within seconds, he was snoring. No one could see him from outside. If anyone stood near the bus, they would be able to hear the snores. At teatime, everyone started looking for Pandu.

When Pandu was nowhere to be found, his elder brother started shouting, "Go look for him in the rehearsal room. Everyone in town is slavering after that actress. He must have gone there too."

Pandu's daughter, who had climbed into the bus to

play hide-and-seek with her friends, started to cry out, "Baba, Baba!"

Pandu dragged himself out of his slumber and sat up suddenly, not knowing where he was. It was evening. It was getting dark inside the bus. Pandu felt afraid and cried out to his daughter, "Soni! Soni! Switch on the lights in the bus!"

"How to do that?" asked Soni.

Pandu sat in the driver's seat, putting his daughter on the hood next to him. Seen from inside the bus, the houses, the village, the mango grove, the darkening skies, they all looked strange. Calling out to his daughter, he jumped off the bus. In the dimming light, the bus looked like a huge two-story building that had suddenly raised its head in the village. A small nameless fear began to rear inside Pandu. "Jueebai," he said, rushing to the rehearsal room.

In her room, the actress was wearing only her petticoat and blouse. She was fanning herself. "It is so hot in this town of yours! You should have brought some cool breezes and some rain in that bus."

Pandu preened. "Dinner . . ." he began to say.

"Will you organize performances for my tamasha company in Mumbai? Only then will I come to your house," the actress said, laughing heartily.

"Sure, sure," said Pandu, showing his teeth.

"Don't be scared, sweetie. I'll come to dinner. And after that you must take me down to the river in your bus."

Right in front of him, she quickly wrapped a shiny sari around herself. Pandu felt happy walking alongside her, seeing that she was dressed grandly for a Ganesh puja and dinner. He was also enthused by Kuwalekar whispering to him that the actress was coming to his house even though many others had invited her.

At Pandu's house, the bhajan was nearly over and the aarti was beginning. Pandu avidly watched the actress clapping her hands and singing an aarti song. The curl on her forehead, the small wrinkle next to her lips, the stain of sweat under her armpits, and her arousing perfume wafting through the house—Pandu seemed lost in these, and his wife did not fail to notice. But she couldn't do anything because she was busy bringing the plates filled with the offering from the kitchen to the puja.

As soon as the aarti was over, Pandu said to the boy playing the harmonium, "Black two," to get the right pitch, and began to sing "Paravashathaa paasha daivi." Watching the middle-aged Pandu sweating like a kabaddi player as he sang his heart out to gain her attention, Jueebai melted. She went and sat next to him, shaking her head from side to side in appreciation. All the women of the house, who were inside arranging banana leaves in a row for dinner, came out to watch. Pandu sang all the verses twice over, and finally when Jueebai joined in, Pandu reached such a height of happiness that he just clutched her hand and fell silent. Feeling that something was going on that shouldn't be allowed, Pandu's elder brother called out to all the guests to take their places for dinner. Pandu's wife, who had witnessed the climax of his duet with the actress, felt as though her domestic bliss and her wifehood had gone up in flames. She began to hit the plates with her ladle as she served everyone. "Eat your rice, eat your rice," she said loudly to Pandu.

After dinner, when Jueebai got up to leave, Pandu introduced her to everyone in his family. He was glad to see that she had kissed his daughter, Soni, on the cheek. Pandu's sister-in-law was looking carefully at how the actress had draped her sari, how her hair was tied, and what jewelry she wore. Even though he called her many times, Pandu's wife did not come out. His elder brother, whose mustache Jueebai had praised, now had a change of heart and said, "Please come to dinner tomorrow also," and wagged his tail all the way to the door.

"I'll drive you home in the bus," said Pandu, and immediately several people climbed on too.

"I'll go onto the upper deck," said Jueebai. "Soni, come sit with me." Saying this, she boarded the bus as though it were an airplane.

The bus went round the maidan a couple of times and then set out for the temple, swaying a little on the dirt road. Pandu's wife had been sulking in the bathroom, hoping someone would persuade her to eat dinner, but since no one had come, she eventually came out, and saw that the bus had gone. She felt unburdened, as though a demon had vanished. But she couldn't forget her husband holding the actress's hand in surrender. "Let him come back—I'll sing a theater song for him all right," she said, gnashing her teeth.

When the bus emptied out at the temple, Pandu did not feel like taking it back home just yet. He sent Soni back with Kuwalekar and stayed behind to rehearse. He couldn't focus on the dialogues he was supposed to learn. And as though things weren't bad enough, Jueebai glowed like a sixty-watt bulb. Every now and then she looked affectionately at Pandu. When she called out, "Pasha, Pasha," a bearded man came up to offer her betel nut, or paan, or her towel. When the rehearsal was over around midnight, everyone was yawning—except Jueebai, who looked as fresh as she had that morning. Not once had Pandu seen her yawn. She seemed to sit there as though she was the source of the boundless energy and spirit he was looking for. He felt like sitting in front of her and singing once more. As the others were leaving, Jueebai stood in front of Pandu and said, "Come, let's go for a ride in your bus. You don't drive, Pasha will. You sit with me."

The big bus came out of the tiny street and began to move slowly in the dark. Jueebai sat in the first seat on the top deck. Pandu sat in the seat next to her. Below, Pasha drove in solitude. Above were rushing clouds and a cool breeze. "Don't look at the sky. You may see the crescent moon and be accused of being a thief tomorrow," laughed Jueebai.

Pandu smiled and looked at the sky. There was no sign of the moon in the heap of clouds. The enormous, empty bus was shaking from side to side. The seats were rattling. In the fading light, Jueebai glowed like a candle. Pandu felt like touching her. Just then Jueebai stood up as though she had glimpsed her destination and pulled the bell. The bus came to a halt.

Both of them climbed down. Nearby, the river flowed like a shadow. The sound of water, heard through the buzzing of jewel bugs, was refreshing. The breeze carried the fragrance of the forest. They stood by the water for a long time. Pasha had gone to sleep with his head resting on his arms on the steering wheel. In the unpeopled tranquility, the lit windows of the bus looked out of place. A sob arose from within Pandu and he gripped Jueebai's hand. She stroked his back gently. At that, Pandu took both her hands and held them to his head as he wept loudly. "Shh," she said, glancing at the bus.

A strange little creature of the forest—squirrel or mongoose—had entered the bus and was looking out at them, blinking. It looked at the sleeping Pasha and then ran away. Jueebai seemed to have melted into the perfume from the forest. Pandu was dumbstruck by how she appeared to understand all his woes and console him silently. As he began to stammer, "This bus . . ." she put a finger to his lips and whispered, "Leave it to me."

In the dark, a breeze came as if to take away the trees, and they shook their heads violently as if to say they did not want to go.

Slowly Jueebai went to the driver's door and tapped on it to awaken Pasha, and said something. In the small cabin, Pasha raised his hands and punched the skies as though he had found a treasure, and turned the key in the ignition. Jueebai stepped back. Filled with light, the double-decker bus started to move. Feeling as if he had received a new lease of life, Pandu went and stood close to Jueebai. They stood and watched the bus until it became a dot of light in the distance. Then, in the cool breeze, they started walking toward the village. After they had walked for a long time, Pandu said suddenly, "My daughter, Soni, is really bright. But she says she doesn't want to go to school. All she wants to do is watch TV at the neighbor's. You must have a word with her."

"Chauthi Chandra," 1995

TOOFAN MAIL

"Maa used to wake me up while it was still dark. She would make me wash my face without making any noise. Then, locking the door of the kholi without switching on a light, she would hold our plastic slippers in her hand and we would walk silently till the end of Teli Galli. When we reached the main road, we would put on our slippers and run all the way to Andheri Station. There we would buy tickets, jump into the first local that came by, and get off at Dahisar. I would feel a strange and helpless joy at the thought of seeing my father. Maa would keep saying 'shhh' to me even though I hadn't spoken. As though responding to her 'shhh,' the entire world seemed to have fallen silent, and in that silence the 'shhh' sounded even louder than it actually was. When it was about to turn four forty-five a.m., both of us would feel a little tense. The Toofan Mail coming from the north would approach at a thunderous speed. It would pass through this deserted station, creating a whirlwind of straw and dust, and disappear in less than a minute.

"The train didn't stop here. But my father would jump from it, a packet tied to his stomach. Rolling onto the platform in a hideous contortion, he stood up before the dust had cleared, threw his bag toward us, and walked away limping, toward the two men waiting at the end of the platform. When he fell onto the platform, we were not to go near him. Until the Toofan Mail's red tail lights had vanished in the distance, until after he had scrambled up, thrown the bag at us, waved sketchily, and disappeared, we stood like carved statues. Then Maa would run and pick up the bag. If I opened my mouth, she would start shushing me again. When we got back to Teli Galli, it would be just waking up. Closing the door behind us, Maa would quickly pull out things from the bag: new clothes, food, metal toys, and money wrapped in plastic and tied with string. This, Maa would immediately put into our trunk. I don't know when she counted the money. Even if she felt happy, she would pretend not to be. It was as though she was always hiding something from our neighbors.

"Why didn't my father come home? What was in the packet tied to his stomach? Who were those people he went away with? Why didn't he get off like the other passengers at Dadar Station where the train stops, instead of jumping off so dangerously at this deserted station? The only response I got from Maa to these questions was once again a 'shhh.' My father's face remained clearly etched in my mind for many days, even though I had seen him only in that half minute as he waved to us and limped away. It frightened me to think there was never a smile on that face. I saw my father six or seven times in this fashion. He never came home. Maa used to go once a week to the station on the designated day. She started going alone and always returned empty-handed. The enormous iron train still thundered by, creating its whirlwind. But no shape now jumped from it. Finally, Maa used to search the platform to see if a bag had been thrown out. After years of waiting, she too passed away. The Toofan Mail kept on tearing through the night. One day I changed my name, which was Munna, to Toofan. This made me feel that my father the brave adventurer and the mother who raised me fearlessly were both with me."

At this point, the stunt artiste Toofan stopped speaking. On the ship, some feet away from the shore, a large glass set was being assembled by the unit boys. Madhuvanti, who had been listening avidly to Toofan's story, now gazed at the set.

The fight scene was being shot in an abandoned mill in Colaba. In yet another part of the mill compound, a dance scene was being rehearsed. Madhuvanti, one of the dancers in the group, had heard that Toofan was doing a bike-jump and glass-break scene, and came running to watch. Six years ago when she had entered into a love marriage with Fighter Baldev, Toofan had been their primary supporter. So whenever Madhuvanti found herself on location shooting with Toofan, she would come to him to relate all her minor domestic sorrows and triumphs. Today she had come to tell him something important, but in the face of the glass-break set she had felt a little scared to talk to Toofan. Usually a glass-break meant that the artiste drove his motorbike through a big sheet of glass. Toofan was considered of late to be a glass-break expert. In today's shot, he was to drive on the deck of the ship, then ride right through the glass set and shatter it with his bike leaping over the water and onto the shore ten feet away.

The water looked rough, and everyone was anxious about the shot. Madhuvanti had kept silent, but Toofan said, "Hey, Madhu, you keep asking me how I came to be named Toofan, so let me tell you my story." As if he would not get a chance to speak to her again, and as though uncovering a hidden wound, Toofan told her about his father and the train. Looking at Toofan, who sat wearing his armor—his chest, arms, shoulders, and pelvis covered—looking like a robot, Madhuvanti did not know how to respond. Toofan laughed and patted her on the back, saying, "Go now, the dance mistress is blowing her whistle. Until your heroine comes, you have to go one-two-three-four, one-two-three-four. Go on now, do your drill."

"Your friend Baldev is eating my life," said Madhuvanti. "Tell you later. Do you know that all of

Sunil Shetty's films are flopping? People only want love stories now. Not much demand for fighting. Even the little work he can get, Baldev won't take up because there's no insurance, no medical bills paid. Why should I risk my life for nothing, he says. So he's just sitting around at home. I'll tell you everything later. Don't forget to take the non-veg lunch. I know you don't eat meat, but I can pack it for home. My little Soni loves the unit's non-veg."

When she stood up, her stomach looked swollen in the ghagra choli she was wearing, and Toofan asked, "So production number two is on the way, is it? Baldev is now doing bedroom scenes, is he?"

Madhu dug him in the ribs. "Don't you think I've anything better to do? Just to bring up the one kid I have to shake my bottom a hundred times a day wearing this dreadful costume in the heat," she said laughing. "I guess I'll work as long as I can. I'm ready to go to Ooty or wherever for outdoor shooting too. Let Baldev look after the house. We need to put Soni into an English-medium school . . ."

As Madhu ran to the dance field, her forced sprightliness seemed an attempt to reduce her real age as she tried to stay in work as a dancer. Toofan felt sorry for her as he saw her joining the line of fifty dancers swaying to the dance mistress's whistle.

Toofan was in the habit of drinking a lime soda before a shot. When the unit boy asked whether he should open the bottle, Toofan told him to wait. Mahale the makeup man whispered in Toofan's ear: "How much have you asked them for this shot? Just twenty thousand like always? Remember this isn't simply a glass-break. You're also jumping over the waves. You must ask for double. Most probably you'll have to spend the entire twenty thousand on hospital charges. And then you'll be eating hospital bread for weeks, with bandages and plaster around you. It's not yet too late. Ask for double. They won't be able to get anyone else to do the glass-break. At least ask for thirty. Go on . . ."

Toofan flew into a rage. "Chup re. Quiet! Do you think I'm a Kennedy Bridge girl who increases her rate when she's touched? A deal is a deal. I've already agreed to do it." He moved his arms around in a circular motion to loosen his shoulder muscles.

Mahale was not exaggerating. After each glass-break, there was always a hospital period where he recuperated from his wounds. When he had broken a bone as the double for Shah Rukh Khan in *Baadshah*, the star himself came incognito one night to see him in his kholi in Teli Galli. No one else from the industry had bothered to ask after him. This was how this line was. One astonishing glass-break, followed by a stretch away from the industry. Toofan had asked himself again and again: Where was the real fun of this bike business? In the strange emptiness that filled his mind before a shot? Or the lightness of the aftermath? Or the thoughtless vulnerable moment of the stunt itself? Madhuvanti's husband, Baldev, was of the opinion that surviving a stunt was the real fun, that before the mind knows you've survived it's the body that knows, and that's the asli fun. Whenever Baldev said that, Toofan felt the Toofan Mail passing through his body. He saw his father again, getting slowly to his feet, limping off in a dignified way, in the full knowledge that he had carried out his duty to perfection.

As Toofan stared at the distance between the ship and the shore, he heard a huge noise in the distance. He turned to see Madhuvanti shouting as she ran toward him. Chasing her, and also shouting loudly, was her husband, Baldev. It seemed like a monitor rehearsal of a scene. People on the sets began to run after them to see the tamasha. Toofan observed that this drama was moving toward him, and soon enough the two, followed by a crowd of spectators, stood gasping in front of him.

"Go on, go on. You're always threatening to tell Toofan. Go on, tell him in front of me," said Baldev, pushing his wife.

Toofan in his mechanical-man outfit waved his hands, asking them to lower their voices: "Arre, arre, shhh, shhh, speak softly. What's all this in front of everyone?" He raised his eyebrows as if to indicate to everyone that he would deal with this.

Without even waiting for the crowd to disperse, Baldev shook his wife, saying, "Go on, go on."

"Toofan, he's been getting at me in the house every single day, and now he's on the sets chasing me. Besharam, shameless hussy is what he keeps on calling me. Last night my five-year-old, Soni, asks: 'Mummy, what is sharam? Why don't you have sharam?' What should I tell her?" Madhuvanti started sobbing.

"This is what I meant. Look at her, crying shamelessly in front of everyone," whined Baldev, clenching his teeth.

When Toofan said, "Enough, stop it," both her weeping and his abuse quietened down.

"Sorry, Toofan," said Madhuvanti. "You have your life-and-death jump now, we shouldn't be distracting you like this. But this idiot was hiding there, looking at my rehearsal. Tell me—am I doing chori and stealing something here that he should be keeping an eye on me? Please, Baldev, let's talk later, let him finish the glass-break," she added as she turned to go.

"Stop!" shouted Baldev. "Toofan, you don't know . . . every day she acts a role in front of me. If I pull her close, she pretends to be shy. Just like the scene of the heroine on her first night, closing her eyes when the hero is slipping off the pallu from her head. She thinks I don't understand. All false. False coyness. It's some dream of becoming a heroine. Every night she enacts this scene. She's a three-paisa extra—that's what she is, not a heroine. Throwing dust in her own husband's eyes." Madhuvanti sat with her hands covering her face.

Not knowing where to look, Toofan stared at the
ships in the far distance. Then he started tightening the
nuts and bolts of his metal footwear for want of anything
better to do. The silence seemed to calm down Baldev
in his attempt to make his private sorrows public and
thereby make them legitimate. He opened his mouth
again: "I've been watching you all this time. When that
fat woman blows her whistle, you start heaving your
chest without a dupatta. You stop when she tells you
to. And when she blows the whistle again you go one-
two-three-four again. When she says faster, you shake
even more."

Not able to listen to this anymore, Madhuvanti
glared at him and said, "That's my job. My job, do you
hear?"

"Then why are you so shy at home? Is that fake or is
it real?" Suddenly Baldev felt he wasn't able to express
what he felt. He waved his hands about but still couldn't
speak. Then the tears came.

"Arre, Baldev, you're a fighter, how can you become
emotional like this?" said Toofan.

Baldev leaned against Toofan's metal shoulder and
cried.

All the light boys came running, shouting, "Baldev
is crying! Baldev is crying!"

Pale but trying to laugh, Madhuvanti said, "What
kind of a man would spy on his wife? Look at him now,
crying like Meena Kumari." She whispered fiercely in

Baldev's ear: "Try not to be shameless in public at least," and pulled him away from Toofan.

Some of the unit men persuaded Baldev to go to the canteen with them. Madhuvanti shook out the pleats of her Rajasthani ghagra skirt and smoothed it down. "Toofan, good luck," she said, shaking his hand. "Afterwards let's all go and eat some kheema pav." Trying to inject liveliness into her every step, holding up her skirt a little, she ran heavily toward her dance troupe. As he looked at her, Toofan suddenly remembered Maa, who used to wake him before dawn to get him ready for the lightning glimpse of his father. Maa must have been the same age as this Madhuvanti then. Toofan felt a peculiar anguish. What was the nature of Madhuvanti's shyness that was so disturbing to Baldev? His mother who seemed so elderly to him in memory—was she really only as old as Madhuvanti? What was her battle for shame, then? Sometimes when his bike slipped during a take, and he fell down, and then stood up slowly with the unit boys lending a hand to straighten the bike, in that silence did he ever feel shame? *Madhuvanti doesn't feel humiliated when she has to shake her bosom in a tight blouse in front of a thousand people, but feels so when Baldev watches her from his hiding place and then abuses her? My lonely mother's constant whispering of "shhh"—was that the voice of her shame, her lonely battle for dignity?*

Toofan began to move slowly toward the shore. There had been no iota of shame in his mother and

himself when they stood unblinking, watching his father fall from the train like an animal that had been
flung out. Or had the Toofan Mail whisked away their
shame? Or is it that a profession, chosen for the living it
afforded, acquired a dignity of its own?

"Shot ready!" called out a voice. Huge lamps lit even
in this sunlight. Boys ran hither and thither as though
preparing for a battle. An ambulance and a stretcher
stood waiting at the far end of the field. The spot boy
opened the bottle of soda and squeezed a lime into it.
After drinking it, Toofan walked across the temporary
plank to reach the ship's deck.

The plank was removed. Toofan climbed onto his
bike. The spot where he was supposed to land had been
marked with white chalk powder. He could hear the
sound of the dance song wafting toward the ship. The
sound of the yellow generators, too. As soon as he put
on his helmet, the sounds became distant. The entire
shore seemed to recede into a deep shyness. Toofan
checked to see how much distance he would need to
cover before he did the glass-break. When the red signal flashed, he drew himself up and kicked the bike's
starter. All of a sudden, he could hear the sound of the
Toofan Mail eating up the distance.

"Toofan Mail," 2002

WATER

"WE WILL BE LANDING AT MUMBAI AIRPORT IN APPROXI-
mately twenty minutes. Please fasten your seat belts."
Chandrahas felt that the plane was shaking a little more
than usual. He looked over his reading glasses at the
skies outside. By this time, he should have been able to
see Khandala, Matheran, Karla, and Lohagad through
a thin curtain of clouds. By this time, he should have
been remembering some picnic, some trek, some trip
or training camp he had been to in the mountains below with fondness. The Karla waterfall, which had once
frightened his friends and him during the monsoon,
should be visible from here like a small metal badge.
But he could see nothing except a thick wall of cloud.
And the aircraft was swinging alarmingly from side to
side. Chandrahas wondered if the plane could land under these conditions. He looked around at his fellow
passengers with a small face as the plane gave a jolt, and

the voice announced: "We apologize for the turbulence caused by inclement weather. Please return to your seats and keep your seat belts fastened." Like a passenger in the last seat of a bus that had just gone over a pothole, the elderly man seated next to Chandrahas said, "My goodness." Chandrahas gave the man's hand a squeeze and smiled at him reassuringly.

In the last ninety minutes, the two had spoken more than was perhaps necessary, and now an artificial silence prevailed. The man's name was Santoshan. He was a Malayali who had lived all over India, and had spent the last thirty years in Ahmedabad establishing his own factory. For the past two years he had been living with his only daughter in Bangalore. He hadn't been well of late, and he came to Mumbai regularly to consult with a famous doctor. Normally his daughter or his son-in-law accompanied him. Today, the son-in-law had been delayed, and was going to be on the next flight. Not wanting to trouble the old man with the tired voice, Chandrahas said, "You'll certainly get well soon. I can see it from your eyes."

Smiling, the old man said, "Tell me the truth and I will believe you. I never used to trust anyone when I was in business. Only believed in money. But after I fell sick, I've started believing anything anyone says."

Santoshan, though, did not seem to want to know anything about his neighbor. Feeling awkward, Chandrahas offered: "I'm from Honnavar, on the west coast of Karnataka. I've been working in Mumbai for the past ten years. I've had an interview for a better job in Bangalore. They even paid for my travel. I'll get twice my present salary. It's as though I've already got the job. But now I don't know what to do."

"Relax, man," said Santoshan. "Stay wherever you can work well. And everything else will take care of itself. Whether it's Timbuktu or Miami or Mumbai, or anywhere else on earth, if you get the right atmosphere and you can lose yourself in your work, it's like you're serving your own country and your town. And if you stay in your own state or town and remain lazy or corrupt or wicked, that's the biggest betrayal." Wishing Chandrahas well, the old man dropped off to sleep, and had woken only now, when the plane was jolted by the storm. Chandrahas guessed that he must be worrying about his son-in-law joining him and how the rains might disrupt their schedules. "Don't worry," he said. The air hostesses were moving up and down the aisle checking to see whether all the passengers had fastened their seat belts. "Whenever there's turbulence, I look at the faces of the air hostesses. If they look normal, fine. But if they look as though they're trying to hide something, then we can expect the worst. But look, this one is smiling . . ."

Santoshan gestured with his head. The noise from the aircraft increased, and it began its descent. Everyone held their breath as the plane plunged and finally thudded onto the runway. As if mocking their fearful journey, Mumbai Airport stood glowing in the bright afternoon sun as though under a spotlight. The passengers jostled one another in their hurry to get off the plane. Santoshan tried to move aside for Chandrahas to alight. But Chandrahas said, "I'm not in a hurry, sir. If you like, I'll stay with you until your son-in-law arrives."

"Really?" asked the old man, pausing. Then he went on: "Do me a favor, then. I doubt that the next flight will arrive on time in this weather. Instead of waiting for my son-in-law, I should go straight to the hospital. My appointment is at three p.m. If it's on your way, you could drop me there and carry on."

"Certainly,' said Chandrahas.

"An autorickshaw will do," said Santoshan, but Chandrahas hailed a taxi and they both got in. The passing vehicles were gleaming, as though the airport was the only spot where it wasn't raining.

"Whatever you might think, sir, once one has stayed in Mumbai for a while, and one comes back after a journey, there's a strange sense of security. Look at the taxi and auto chaps here, they always return your change, however little it is. There's something that welds us all together here," said Chandrahas, as he pulled his water bottle out of his bag and gave it to Santoshan, asking him to drink. As the old man guzzled, the veins in his neck shone. Seeing the brown radiation burn marks on his neck, Chandrahas mentally wished the man a quick recovery.

"You're quite right. I, too, wanted to set up my business in Mumbai, and I even stayed here for some time. But the girl I lost my heart to was from Ahmedabad, and she wasn't ready to leave that town. Like in that story about the king who went on a hunt and heard the voice of a bird, and for its sake acquired the branch, the tree, the grove, and the entire region, and he set up his kingdom there and never went home." Santoshan spoke to the taxi driver, asking him, "And you, my man, have you ever been in love?"

The driver laughed. "Parvadta nahi, saab, can't afford it." Encouraged by his passengers' conversation, he went on: "Money flows like water in Mumbai, saab. Some see it, some don't. Those who see it grab it by the handful, and travel by taxi. Those who don't, become taxi drivers."

"No, no," said Chandrahas, "there are also people like me who see the money but can't get hold of it."

The taxi driver, who said his name was Kunjbihari, pointed to the sky, which now looked like a black wall. "Look at that, sir, a lot of water will fall today, bahut paani girne wala hai," he said.

Chandrahas was always amused by the Mumbai idiom that referred to rain as "water falling." He thought of the Holi festivities, when someone in the apartment above would throw buckets of colored water on the revelers below. As the taxi climbed onto the overpass after Santacruz, the skies darkened even more. "See, Kunjbihari, plenty of money is collecting in the sky," said Santoshan.

Asking the driver to wait outside Hinduja Hospital, Chandrahas went in with Santoshan to meet Dr. Dastur, the specialist. Not heeding Santoshan's protests, Chandrahas insisted on waiting with him. He phoned his wife, Sarayu, who worked in an office at Churchgate, and told her, "It looks like it's going to rain very heavily. You should leave the office early. I'll be home in a couple of hours . . . Yes, I know, we have to pay our loan installment today. Let's do it tomorrow, please. It doesn't matter . . . I don't know, I think I've got the job . . . Yes, yes, I've told them I'll need to be given a house . . . No, we need to decide now. I'm finding it difficult . . . Sarayu, you tell me what to do. How long can we struggle here just because we like the city?" He hung up after whispering goodbye.

Santoshan thumped him on the back and said, "Good, do as she says."

Just then, Santoshan's name was called. He picked up his file and asked Chandrahas whether he would accompany him. After examining the old man behind a drawn curtain, Dr. Dastur proclaimed, "Excellent, Mr. Santoshan. You're doing very well. The treatment from your doctor in Bangalore seems to be okay. Maybe you need to finish another cycle of radiotherapy, but you can do that there. Why didn't your daughter come? How is she? How is the school that she's running?" As he spoke, the doctor wrote out the details of his examination on his letterhead.

Then for the first time, Chandrahas saw a deep helplessness in Santoshan's demeanor. The old man, dragging his voice out from deep down, said, "Doctor saab, sir . . ."

"Yes, what is it?" asked the doctor as he kept on writing.

"Nothing really, just that next April my granddaughter might get married—it is being planned right now."

"My God . . . You have a granddaughter about to be married? Unbelievable! Well, I'll see if I can find a seminar to go to in Bangalore, and be sure to attend the wedding."

"So kind of you, Doctor. But that's not what I meant . . ."

"Then?"

"It's only another six months. Somehow you must keep me alive until then."

"No, no! You'll live a hundred years."

"I'm sure you tell everyone that. You seem like God when you say that. I want to do nothing else but keep looking at you. But I know what's happening with me . . ."

Just then, Santoshan's son-in-law called. His flight had not yet left Bangalore. "Don't worry, I'm with the doctor. I will call you later," Santoshan said, cutting the call short.

"Doctor, please . . . stretch my life till April. I've promised my granddaughter that I'll be there for her wedding. Please try . . ."

Dr. Dastur gently slapped him as though in anger. "What rubbish! You'll move on only when you've seen your granddaughter's daughter." He looked at Chandrahas as though to seek his approval.

Chandrahas felt a cloud pass over his heart. "I'll wait outside," he said, slipping away. It sounded like a tenant pleading with his landlord to let him stay for another six months. Santoshan's request was intense in its simplicity. Rows and rows of people sat outside, waiting their turn, waiting to make their request. A few months for some, a few days for the others . . .

Then he saw Kunjbihari, the taxi driver, running toward him with some urgency, shouting, "Saab . . . the rain's falling at a tremendous pace! You should leave now, or none of us will get home today. The local trains are slowing down. I hear there's water on the tracks at Sion and Kurla. The traffic is slowing down too. If you need to stay here any longer, I'll leave." He was as alert as an animal that has heard the approach of impending disaster.

Chandrahas reassured him: "No, we'll just be a minute. Where will this uncle go in this weather? Let's take him wherever he wants to go." Chandrahas went inside, and Kunjbihari ran out, finessing the strategy through which he would pull his car out of the maze of honking vehicles.

By the time the taxi came to the main road, day had prematurely turned to night, and water was falling in thick sheets from the skies. The roads were full of vehicles trying to get to the distant suburbs. "Oh, what mazaa this Mumbai rain is!" exclaimed Santoshan.

"Fun? What are you saying? Now you'll see mazaa," Kunjbihari drawled, rubbing his forearms as though he were preparing for battle. Throwing the taxi into little lanes and alleys, he began to take them toward Mahim Creek.

"You can drop me anywhere. I have friends at Bandra Bandstand. They'd come and fetch me," said Santoshan.

"No one will come," said Kunjbihari. "Everyone is stuck somewhere. Like us. Look at this . . . we're khalaas, finished!" He beat his forehead and pointed to the jam on the Mahim-Bandra overpass. Vehicles were stuck to one another like thousands of ants, showing no sign of movement. In the deafening and blinding rain, the city itself appeared to be melting away. From their vantage point on the bridge, Kunjbihari's passengers could see the local trains below, at a standstill on the flooded tracks. Some of the braver passengers had jumped into the waist-high water and seemed to be swimming hither and thither. People had alighted from stationary buses and were trudging on foot toward their destinations.

"In another hour, the rain will stop and everything will be fine."

"In another two hours, the police will set right the traffic."

Chandrahas was tired of saying these words again and again. Over the taxi's FM radio, they were hearing news of how the entire city had come to a standstill. There were also messages from people to their families, to their children, to their friends, relayed by the radio station:

"Where are you?"

"You must stay back in the office."

"I'll go to my maami's place."

"I'm fine."

"I'll stay on the station platform."

By this time, water had filled the electric grids and the telephone control boxes, and the city's phone lines fell silent. Chandrahas tried to call Sarayu several times from his mobile but failed. Maybe she was still at her office. Maybe she was at Churchgate Station in a train car. Maybe she was walking through waterlogged streets. Thinking of this made him more silent.

"Don't worry," said Santoshan. "She is sure to be safe." As he spoke, he realized that his son-in-law wasn't going to be able to reach him. "Kunjbihari, do one thing. Drop me back at the airport. I have a return ticket. I'll just take whatever flight I can get."

"We can't go anywhere without the traffic moving, saab," said the driver, getting out of the taxi and splashing ahead in the water to see what was happening.

Now night started mingling with the darkness of the rain. The phalanx of rainwater poured down as if to mix up all the colors of old images. Even those travelers who had ten or twelve miles to go were getting off stranded buses into the water, and slowly a mass of people began to move around the vehicles. Everywhere in the city, the water was rising swiftly. *The same clouds that shook our aircraft this afternoon are now breaking into pieces*, thought Chandrahas. Then the clouds had seemed like a battalion of tanks ranged for war. Chandrahas wondered what kind of turbulence this heedless rain was evoking in the poor old man who wanted just another six months on this earth.

"Sir, shall I get us something to eat? Keep listening to the radio, I'll be back soon," said Chandrahas as he got out of the taxi and walked toward the Mahim market. There was a curious spirit in the crowds that walked along, soaked with rain. Some were whooping and shouting. They were calling out to those still in vehicles, heckling them:

"This bus won't move today."

"The entire highway is underwater."

"Mahim Creek is flooding."

"The seawater is getting into the low-lying areas."

"The ground floors of all the houses in Kalanagar have been flooded."

As the crowd muttered to itself, these bits of information spread to everyone in the city. Schoolchildren in their uniforms in the pouring rain, with soaking schoolbags, walked like small, bent mountaineers in the darkness. Where did they live? How would they get there? When would they reach? Shopkeepers were calling out to the children and handing them biscuits, bread, and bananas. People in the area were asking the children to come into their homes and wait out the rain. Neighboring chawls and apartments were opening their doors to the women and children getting off buses. Chandrahas bought chips and some bananas and strode back to the taxi through the water. Santoshan had just finished talking to Kunjbihari. "There's a traffic jam until Borivali, saab. And all the vehicles trying to take short cuts through the suburbs have caused an even bigger jam. The water is too high to recede quickly. Or else I would have told you to start walking. You could have reached the airport in an hour, and at least got some shelter over your heads. But no, my Basanti's your only refuge today."

"Basanti?"

"My taxi's name, saab."

"Where's your house, Kunjbihari?"

"Not a house, saab. Just a kholi—in Oshiwara. My wife and children are far away, in Uttar Pradesh state. Only if I drive a taxi here will they be able to light a fire in the house."

Suddenly Santoshan asked, "Kunjbhai, does life seem to you like hell or like heaven?"

"What a time to ask this question, saab!" said Kunjbihari. "But look, how people are enjoying themselves even at this time—as though this was a fairground. Well, everything depends on how we think about it. If I think I'm happy, it's happy I am. If I think I'm sad, then I'm sad. Isn't that so, saab?"

As if to say how simple and right the driver's philosophy was, Santoshan raised his eyebrows at Chandrahas. Kunjbihari went on, "As someone said—it's better to be happy in hell than unhappy in heaven." He settled down to eat a banana.

On the radio, they could hear that all forms of transport—planes, trains, buses—had been canceled. There were also these announcements:

"For Pankaj, Shweta, and Nobin, who are stuck at Dadar TT, this special song . . . 'Kajra Re'!"

"On the request of Jyoti Patel and her friends stuck in a train between Ghatkopar and Vidyavihar stations for the past six hours, we're playing 'Dil Chahta Hai.'"

Thus, even under pressure the city was sharing its songs.

"Amma, I'm staying at my aunt's house in Shivaji Park. Don't worry about me, I'll come home tomorrow. But don't get angry with me—my schoolbag fell into a drain near Portuguese Church." When they heard this boy's message, Santoshan breathed the word *Amma*.

Something seemed to affect Chandrahas, who swallowed hard and then began to speak: "Sir, I must share this story with you. A couple, our close family friends, had two lovely children. Suddenly, three years ago, the husband died of an illness. The widow was trying hard to raise the children, but just four months ago her daughter died in an accident. Now she's completely shattered. She thinks everyone she loves is likely to leave her. She's afraid that if she loves her eight-year-old son too much, he'll go away too. So she's always cold and rude to him. One day this child says to her, 'Amma, since Pepsi is supposed to have pesticide in it, why don't you and I slowly drink two large bottles of it and kill ourselves?' How can an eight-year-old kid think of committing suicide? How can we reduce their pain, sir? Why should they experience such suffering?"

It was past midnight. Throughout the city, the vehicles had come to a standstill. Those who were in buses and trains went to sleep in their seats. Those in offices, shops, and kiosks dozed where they sat. Those who had started walking found that they couldn't go any farther, or couldn't go back to their starting point either. Hotels kept their shutters open, allowing passersby to come inside and sleep. Sardarjis had set up free kitchens wherever possible, and served dal and roti to those who were stranded on the street. But the city's feet were still submerged in water.

Kunjbihari awoke. Opening the door on Santoshan's

side, he said, "Uncle, let's go." Half asleep, the old man slowly got out of the car, and limped along because his feet had gone to sleep. Chandrahas followed them. In this strange, wet night with its intoxicating mixture of sleep and wakefulness, of water, light, fear, journeying, and weariness, they walked as though in a dream. Between them was the feeling of an intimate fatigue, as if they had known each other for a long time. Guiding them through a few small gullies, Kunjbihari brought them to a tumbledown dwelling that seemed half-drowned in the water. A few children were trying to remove whatever water they could with buckets. The cot, a chair, and cupboards were submerged. Standing in the middle of all this, a woman was slapping rotis onto a pan. On various nails hung the possessions of the house—a cloth bag, an umbrella, a clock, and a sari or two.

"Kaanchubehen, I'm Kunjbihari, a friend of Hasmukh Ali, who's a friend of your husband, Pyaremohan's. I've never visited you all before. Today, when the entire city's gone phut, we got stuck by Mahim Creek."

"Please sit down. Have some roti," said the woman, giving them each a plate with two rotis. They stood in the water and ate in that uncanny silence. The woman's children held out cups of water to them. Chandrahas could not drink it. Santoshan gazed at his cup as if meditating, and then drank the water slowly sip by sip. Chandrahas felt both anxiety and surprise. As they thanked the woman and took their leave, Chandrahas whispered, "Should we give them something?"

"No, no," said Kunjbihari. "Hasmukh Ali would kill me."

"Kaanchubehen," Kunjbihari addressed their host. "You husband was near Colaba this morning around ten. There's not much flooding there. I'm sure he's been getting customers that side. Tomorrow, when the water goes down, he'll come home. Don't worry about him." Before they walked away, Kunjbihari quietly slipped some money into the children's pockets.

When they got back to Basanti in the midst of thousands of stalled vehicles, the rain was still coming down. Some volunteers were directing the walkers: "Go this way. Milan Subway is underwater. And all the drains are open. Try to walk only on the roads." Others were handing bread and fruit to those stuck in their cars. Piercing through the stillness of the night, a train standing in the water would suddenly let out a whistle. Chandrahas felt very thirsty and couldn't fall asleep. He went to a small grocery shop nearby. Almost everything was sold out. Chandrahas saw a crate of twelve bottles of Bisleri water. When Chandrahas asked the white-haired shopkeeper for water, he was handed one bottle.

"We're two of us," said Chandrahas. "One has to go back to Bangalore. We don't know how long we're going to be stuck here. Why don't you sell me the entire crate? I'll give you double."

The shopkeeper laughed sadly. "Do you think you're the only one stuck on the road? Can't you see? Women, children, old people—they're all stuck. This is all I have. You're a young man and look quite fit. Take just one bottle, and take one more for your friend. Is this a time to make money? Here, give me twenty rupees. That's the printed price."

Chandrahas was filled with shame. Handing over the money, he took the two bottles and returned to the taxi.

They sat for a long time in silence. Much after midnight, when the sound of human beings diminished, the men in the taxi felt as though they were hearing the waves of the sea, which wasn't far. Around the streetlights one could see the drops of rain falling. Kunjbihari said, "Don't worry, sir. I'll pray that you get well soon. You'll certainly be there for your granddaughter's wedding. This is my prayer for you this night."

Santoshan squeezed the driver's shoulder, saying, "You know why I got this sickness? I was one of the first in this country to sell water. In the 1970s, I was the first to bottle water and sell it. My mind was telling me not to, but I did it all the same. You said earlier that money flows like hidden water, but I sold the water that was before my eyes. The happiness you get from doing what's right is nothing compared to the unhappiness of doing something even while knowing it's wrong. That's a sin. That's why I've fallen sick. It's my body punishing me for not listening to myself. I now have to experience this—there's no way out."

As Santoshan stared out of the window, an orange thrown by a volunteer fell into his lap, and he held it with both hands, laughing, like a kid taking a catch. "Kunjbhai, the rotis you got us today and the water we drank are the tastiest things I've eaten in my entire life. It was like amrit."

Old Hindi film songs wafted from the FM radio stations as did more messages. Every now and then, Santoshan kept stroking Chandrahas's hand, saying, "Don't worry about Sarayu. She must have paid the loan installment and got onto the local train. She'll be fine, wherever she is. There can't be a safer time than this."

"Yes, sir, there isn't a safer place than this right now. This city never lets go of your hand. As Sarayu said, I'll continue in my present job and stay in Bombay." Kunjbhai turned down the radio volume and tried to sleep with his head on the steering wheel. Suddenly, they heard a weird voice. A man pushing along a small bicycle was shouting, "Amitabh Bhaiyya zindabad, Amitabh Bhaiyya amar rahe, long live." Behind him were a dozen people also pushing cycles, flying colorful flags. They carried bags, a small bucket, and a few other things tied to their cycles, giving the impression that they were on a long journey. Chandrahas and Kunjbihari got out of the vehicle and waited for the procession to go past. In the dead of night, in those waterlogged and weary streets, the man's followers kept proclaiming the heroic journey's purpose.

"Our Gagan Bhaiyya has come all the way from Allahabad. He's a born fan of Amitabh Bachchan. When he heard that his hero's health is not good, he took a vow so that Bachchanji can get well again. Because of that vow, he's brought water from the Ganga-Yamuna sangam, bringing it all the way on a bicycle. We believe that if a person drinks this water he'll be cured of all ailments. But look at this magic! We bring the water all the way on a cycle for thousands of miles, and the moment we reach this city the skies break open! What a good omen. Move aside, let us pass! Amitabh Bhaiyya zindabad, long live! Amitabh Bhaiyya amar rahe!" On Gagan Bhaiyya's face there was supreme joy. The sangam water swished around in his little vessel. The movements of his limbs contained the swirl of this water. Kunjbihari called out, "Gagan Bhaiyya, go straight and turn left at Khar, and then go straight to Juhu. That's where Amitabh Bhaiyya's house is."

As the little vessel of sangam water brought for Gagan Bhaiyya's hero went past in the last hour of the night, in this street filled with deep silence after this flood that had marooned lakhs of homes and lakhs of people, Santoshan felt he was witnessing a humble object becoming divine. He said to Chandrahas, "Come in and sleep a little. We've already spent fourteen hours here. Don't know how much longer it'll be."

As Chandrahas sat in the car he said to the driver, "Kunjbhai, you too should go to sleep. Good night."

Kunjbihari began to laugh. "Good night? It's good morning already. Look at that." Slowly, it was becoming light. The predawn glow from the east shone on the thousands of vehicles backed up on the road, giving the illusion that they might start moving at any time.

"Neeru," 2006

PARTNER

As Roopak Rathod stood gripping the poles of the enormous Murphy Baby hoarding glistening blue, pink, and purple in the weak sunlight near Nana Chowk, he felt he suddenly understood everything. Yes, his partner had been lying. He'd certainly got a big job of some kind. No doubt he'd managed to get a huge salary. *But he can't show off his happiness and his grand job in front of me, a useless temporary jobber. So he comes home with a long face. Slowly he's escaping my gaze and moving up to another level alone, without a sound, without giving any inkling as to what he's doing.*

With this sudden flash of knowledge, Roopak felt quite excited, standing on the traffic divider surrounded by vehicles. That whole year they had experienced a sort of semi-employed status, Roopak and his "partner," his roommate in the ten-square-foot room they rented.

The partner was about five years older than Roopak, but gave the impression that he was younger because of his squeaky voice. He had never talked about his job or native town and did not ask Roopak about these things either. Half-jobs, one meal a day, some obvious lies, desires that seemed like the torn posters on the walls of the public park. In their daily lives, there wasn't that much difference, or any secrets to be kept. There was no question of lending and borrowing money, since there was no money at all.

This partner who was never weighed down by words had for over a week now become tight-lipped. He had put a small lock on his suitcase. Sometimes he pretended to be in pain. He never told Roopak what his salary was. He only said it was enough for him to make do with. "Go and have your dinner, I'm not hungry now," he would say, and then go out very late, after the kala-khatta sherbet carts near Chowpatty Beach had packed up for the night, and come back after a large meal, chewing on paan. Earlier, he would shave with the bathing soap, but now he had bought a tube of shaving cream. He'd also bought nice-smelling aftershave lotion to splash on his face after his bath. "You can use it if you like," he would say to Roopak, but never "Here, take this . . ."

Yes, his partner's world was changing. He seemed to be preparing himself for life on another planet. His sentences groped for new words. Earlier, he would speak roughly like they always did—"Tere ku," "Mere ku," "Teri maa ki"—but not now, not in this new role. Roopak suddenly understood his partner's plight. This understanding cast new light on the incident that had taken place just half an hour ago.

Usually, his partner wore a shirt for three or four days, and a pair of pants for a week. Today, he came out of the bathroom, threw his clothes from the previous day into a corner, took out ironed clothes from their *Times of India* wrapping, and put them on. When Roopak looked at him questioningly as though asking, "What's going on?" he suddenly shouted, "Arre, where has it gone? Where's my watch?" He started looking everywhere.

Roopak felt that the partner wasn't casting aspersions on him, but he still felt a strange twinge. He got up to help look, but the partner said, "Why are you searching? I'm the one who put down the watch. You've just come home from work. I don't want to bother you. Go to sleep, go to sleep. My watch, my new watch." He crawled under the cot and began to pull out all the old papers from there. Caught in this strange space between familiarity and contempt, Roopak could not help feeling humiliated.

"Why do you put a new watch here and there? You should have put it in your VIP suitcase," he mumbled.

His partner raised his hands in a dramatic namaste, saying, "Achha, sorry." He put on his shoes and went out, shutting the door behind him.

Unable to bear the silence in the room, Roopak went out and was now standing on the divider in the midst of the traffic, thinking of how funny and pitiable his partner's actions were. Just yesterday, the partner had bought new hangers. Whenever he moved around the room, there was a perfume that wafted along with him. And yes, there were new white rubber slippers. The partner seemed to be hesitant to buy anything that Roopak did not have, but at the same time he appeared to be trying to overcome that hesitation. These white slippers created a storm in that small room. The partner wore them all the time—while washing his hands and feet in the mori or while taking a leak while half-asleep. When the slippers were wet they made a thick slapping sound. Roopak began to feel that his partner's fierce attempt to shrink his world and his equally fierce pain were somehow out of place. He thought it best that he find another place. He had wanted to tell the partner this very evening that he was planning to leave.

Climbing down from the divider, Roopak went into Goodluck Irani Café as usual, and had maska pao and two cups of tea. He then walked toward Chikalwadi, where the kholi was. On the way, he stopped for a few seconds on Kennedy Bridge and looked down at the peak-hour local trains and the first floor of the nearby building where the mujra dancers lived. The pink muslin curtains, the bolsters with their silk covers, the tablas covered with embroidered cloth, the sarangi with its ivory inlay—these lay quiet in the middle of the day. Someone must be dusting in those rooms, because the rising dust motes made the sunbeams brighter. Down in the street, some women were bargaining with the omelette seller. Two women were sitting on the steps, one picking lice from the other's hair. These same women paint their lips pink and dance every night. Roopak and his partner had often come over this bridge, and stopped to stare at the pink curtains. As they listened to the fragments of familiar songs from *Pakeezah*, *Muqaddar Ka Sikandar*, or *Umrao Jaan*, the partner would say, "To go in there, we need lots of money in our pockets. For now, we'll listen from here." Sometimes he even seemed to forget Roopak, who was standing beside him, and stare entranced at the curtains. Seeing them standing there, others too would stop. Nothing could be seen. But each man imagined things. Ears pricked to hear the scraps of song, they stood as though lost to the world. But now everything looked different—like their relationship, which didn't have any clear definition.

Roopak saw the door of the room open and was startled. He ran up and went inside, and saw the partner lying on the bed in his ironed clothes, clutching his stomach.

"What happened?" asked Roopak, approaching him.

"No, don't touch me. My stomach hurts badly," he began to scream.

His face was white, and he was sweating profusely. A couple of neighbors rushed in and insisted that the partner be taken to the doctor immediately. Roopak put him into a taxi, took him to the nearby Bhatia Hospital, and went straight to the Outpatients department. The partner began to weep uncontrollably. When Roopak said, "Don't be afraid, nothing will happen," the partner held his roommate's hand, pulled some money out of his pocket, and gave it to Roopak.

"That's all right, we can deal with this later," said Roopak, even as he thrust the money into his own pocket without looking to see how much it was, though he was worried about the hospital expenses. A nurse wheeled the partner away. Roopak debated whether or not he should follow. The nurse motioned to him that he should come with them.

"Severe appendicitis. We have to operate at once," said the doctor, handing Roopak a form to sign. "Hurry, hurry." Seeing Roopak's signature, the doctor said, "Nice name."

The partner, now lying on a gurney, looked intently at Roopak. The nurse gave Roopak a piece of paper and said, "Get all these medicines."

When he returned, the stretcher was at the door of the operating theater, and the partner was in a green hospital gown. The nurse handed Roopak the partner's pants, shirt, and underwear. Some scraps of paper fell out of the shirt pocket. As Roopak bent down to retrieve them, the partner, already drowsy, said, "Look here, I have a distant relative in Borivali. He has a Xerox shop outside the station. I haven't seen him myself, but he's a relative on my mother's side. A bald chap . . ."

"Let's call him after the operation," said Roopak.

"No, no need to call him. He doesn't know who I am. No point calling him. Only that . . . if something goes wrong during the operation . . . the remaining money and my belongings can be given to him." The green-gowned doctor asked the partner to take off his gold chain. When the nurse tried to remove it, it got stuck, and it was only with much effort from both the doctor and the nurse that they were able to take it off, and it was also handed over to Roopak. The gurney was wheeled inside.

Since they had told him to wait outside until the operation was over, Roopak sat on a bench. The woman sitting next to him was holding a handbill reading "Sari Bumper Reduction Sale" and staring fixedly at it. In front of Roopak's eyes was the partner's tortured face as the gold chain was being pulled over his head. He reached into his pocket, took the chain out, and looked at it. It looked like a tiny pathetic thing. The woman next to him said, "My elder sister's being operated on too. They took her in this morning. Her gold bangle couldn't be removed, so they had to cut it off."

What if the partner dies during the operation? But I'm not even his relative—only his roommate. I don't know anything about it. He said he had a stomachache, so I brought him here. He would say all this and leave. Was this easier? Or would it be easier to look for that bald relative in Borivali?

The woman said, "They're calling you." A nurse was beckoning from the OT door.

When Roopak went to her, walking slowly, she asked if he was "the patient party." A doctor who had removed his green mask showed him something in a small aluminum dish, something that looked like a finger covered with blood. "Look, this is the appendix. It had gone septic," he said. As if to alert Roopak, who was looking dully at the dish, the doctor said, "You've seen it, haven't you?" Roopak nodded. Immediately the doctor and nurse went inside again. The nurse came back saying, "We'll keep him in the post-operative ward for a day. From tomorrow he can be given fruit juice." She handed Roopak another piece of paper with the names of some more medicines scrawled on it.

Roopak came out into the sunlight, and felt that the world around him had no connection with him. Again and again he seemed to see, as if on a white screen, the doctor showing him his partner's appendix just like the barber holds up a mirror to show you the back of your head after a haircut. Again and again he saw himself nodding as though he was approving of the evidence. Roopak had no idea who his partner's mother and father were, or where they were. He didn't know a thing about him, but when he remembered seeing that piece of his intestine, a shiver went through him. He felt choked with emotion. He opened the plastic bag in his hand and looked at the clothes inside. They appeared like children hesitating to go to a stranger. Roopak took out the clothes that had been hastily thrust inside the bag and began to fold them one by one. A railway season pass, a comb, various scraps of paper. Feeling something hard in the pants pocket, Roopak put his hand inside and found a shining new watch. Did the partner forget that morning that he had the watch in his pocket, or had he actually hidden it on purpose? Roopak did not care. That tiny finger of the intestine sitting in the aluminum dish swaddled in cotton, like the supreme form of civil mistrust, had made a secret bond flower within him. The watch was like a toy that children had forgotten they had hidden during play. Its ticking sound could be heard.

Roopak went to the public phone booth and called his factory to say that he wouldn't be able to come in for four days. He purchased the medicines, counted the money that was left, and came to the post-operative ward where they had just brought the partner. In his frock-like gown, on the green sheets, the partner lay in helpless slumber, with various kinds of tubes sticking out of him, for blood and saline, and the wires for the ECG. As Roopak looked at him unblinkingly, the nurse smiled and said using signs, "Everything's fine. Go and have your lunch."

"Partner," 2001

MOGRI'S WORLD

A FTER WALKING FROM THE S HIVAJI N AGAR HUTMENTS IN
Mulund to the train station to catch the eleven a.m.
local to Victoria Terminus, Mogri sprinkles some water
on her face in the public toilet before squeezing past the
tiny shops on the footpath selling toys, fruit, and electronics, and reaches the Light of India Irani restaurant
in an old Victorian building at Flora Fountain just as the
clock strikes one.

The Light of India restaurant is already more than
seventy years old. Its companions have long since
changed their appearance and become shops, show-
rooms, or darkened permit rooms, but the restaurant
with its large, square front door and its white windows,
like those of a hospital, stays open to light and air. Since
it is an old structure, the municipality has required that
the building's pillars be propped up by wooden struts—
like walking sticks. Someone seeing it for the first time

might well imagine the propped-up restaurant to be an old man with a supporting stick, saying that his life was nearly done.

The restaurant is run by three brothers who look alike, and as though they are of the same age. No one knows where they live, or whether they have families. They take turns at the cashier's desk. They talk among themselves in a language only they understand. They have loud fights on the phone. The next second they talk with great courtesy to the customers, almost as though they would even pick up a cigarette that a customer might drop by mistake at a table. At night, when the outer shutters are pulled, the owner waits with a smile until the last customers decide to leave. As though charmed by these courtesies, customers occupy their regular tables and while away their time. Apart from the three brothers, there are, inside the small kitchen, Thambi and Badebhai, both past forty; three waiters all over fifty; and Mogri, who has just joined the staff, and is nearing thirty. Mogri is dark-complexioned, ordinarily attractive. When she writes the bill, she twists her lips slightly.

Mogri did not know where she was born or where she took her first steps. Ever since she could remember, she had lived in the Shivaji Nagar chawl. Her mother was a Kamati woman from Hyderabad, her father a Marathi man from Ratnagiri. They came together as construction laborers, and pulled the shards of their family life together in a hundred unfinished buildings. As the buildings they labored on rose up, they raised Mogri, too. Her mother remembered every under-construction building in which she had swung her daughter's cloth cradle while she worked. In a marble-floored mansion in Chembur, Mogri spoke her first words. The parents spoke to each other only in Marathi, and her father named her Mogri after the Ratnagiri dialect word for the jasmine flower. After Mogri failed her tenth-grade exams, she stopped going to school. Although she had spoken Marathi since childhood, while growing up she spoke a hybrid Hindi like everyone else. She called her mother "Maa," and she could not remember calling her father anything, since there was no reason to address him. All her communication was with her mother, who had also told her that her father had a wife and family in his village in Ratnagiri, in addition to a third one in Jogeshwari. He managed all three families as though it was no big deal. The most he said to Mogri was: "Baby, get me some maawa." The little girl would run to the corner of the chawl and get a small packet of the masala-lime-tobacco mixture from the Shetty stall. This tiny stall displayed all kinds of new commodities: brightly colored hair clips, bejeweled hairpins, rakhis when Raksha Bandhan drew near. At Navratri, on her way with her friends to a ras garba dance organized in the neighboring building, Mogri stopped at the stall to buy two new hair clips. The owner's son, just sprouting a mustache, gave her an extra one, and pinched her hand. Throughout the dancing, the Shetty boy's eyes searched for Mogri as he moved from one vantage point to another. Mogri, wearing her new hair clips, stared for hours at the rich people in their shimmering clothes as they danced in a circle. Stroking his budding mustache, smoothing his hair down, the Shetty boy threw small smiles at Mogri. She would laugh as though she felt shy. As soon as Raksha Bandhan came around, the young people of the neighborhood went wild. All kinds of young men got rakhis tied on to their hands by the girls. It became an occasion to touch hands and bodies. Mogri took her chance and tied a rakhi, bought from his own stall, to the Shetty boy's hand, calling him her "maanlela bhaavu," or "assumed" brother. One afternoon, she went with him to see *Ram Teri Ganga Maili* in the cinema. Whenever the film star Mandakini appeared in a drenched thin white sari, the Shetty boy saw Mogri drenched too. In the darkness of the theater, Mogri became aware of a heavenly freedom inside her. And she felt grateful to the boy who had helped create that awareness.

The boy who behaved so impassively in the shop became the object of competition among several girls who had all tied rakhis on him as maanlela bhaavu. One such girl stole two rupees from her house, bought batata vada in the market, and gave it to the Shetty boy. He ate one of them and gave the rest to another girl with a tickle.

A new building was coming up near the chawls—all the bedrooms, all the kitchens in those apartments were half-finished. There were heaps of sand and cement everywhere. As though operating a rota, the Shetty boy used to take his "sisters" to the half-finished building. "There's a secret treasure there—let me show you," he told each one of them.

On Sundays, or during the Saturday film on TV, or during *Chhaaya Geet*, or during the Ganesh festival week when programs were conducted in the neighborhood every evening, when people's attention was elsewhere, the Shetty boy would tie his lungi and plunge into the unfinished building. The girl would climb in through a different door and the search for the hidden treasure would commence in the damp semi-bedroom with the sand and nails on the floor, piercing their bodies as they lay there. There was also the pervasive smell of wood shavings. Especially when it was raining outside, Mogri felt there was excitement in the very air. The boy started the pleasure machine in her, and then disappeared in a trice. To Mogri he seemed generous to a fault.

But slowly Mogri got tired of the hidden treasure. Without saying anything, she stopped going to the unfinished building. At the same time, her friend Yamuna started experiencing severe stomachaches. When the doctor made sly remarks, Yamuna started weeping loudly. Without worrying about what people might think, she held on to the Shetty boy's hand at the bus stop and said to him: "Anna, my elder brother, you are my only hope." The boy did not fail her. One evening he took Yamuna along with Mogri to the Pearl Centre and spent eighty rupees for the procedure. After making the payment, he rushed off on the pretext of work. Mogri somehow felt that Yamuna should have paid half the money. Then she told herself that Yamuna could not have been able to get the money together, and saluted the generous Shetty boy. It was quite a task for Mogri to bring the wilting Yamuna back in the women's compartment of the local train. The compartment was full of women returning from work, many of them in sleeveless sari blouses with their necks and armpits powdered, some who picked up their sari pallu and fanned themselves with it, some that you thought looked rather nice, and would just then yawn widely and dig her nose. The two girls squeezed themselves into a small space between the women. At one point, someone got up from her seat as her station approached. Mogri tried to plonk Yamuna onto that seat, but a beauty with dark glasses pushed them aside and took the seat. Yamuna felt dizzy, and slumped as she stood. The compartment was plastered with abortion clinic posters, and the women commuters hung grimly on to the rod, clutching handbags to their bosoms. Their right hands looked as though they had been made strong by the daily hanging routine. *What a life for a woman*, thought Mogri. It was perhaps in that train compartment that Mogri outgrew the phase of the hidden treasure, and was catapulted into a different life.

AROUND THAT TIME, MOGRI'S FATHER RECEIVED A POST-card saying that his wife in Ratnagiri was sick, and he went off to see her. Because they didn't have any money now, Amma started to work in a neighborhood building, sweeping and washing dishes. She had helped to build it as a construction laborer, carrying sand and dirt. Now there were hundreds of families there, mostly Gujaratis. Their cooking used a good deal of oil, making the utensils difficult to clean. She was shouted at if she used extra soap. Taking advances from the houses in which she worked, Amma sent money to the other wife in Ratnagiri. Sometimes Mogri would go with her mother to help with the chores, and since she dressed neatly the mistress of the house would cluck: "Cheh, cheh, what a nice girl. And she's been to school. Why do you bring her to do this kind of work?"

When her mother had had her period, Mogri would take her place. And the girls of her age who sat painting their nails in the chawl looked down on her. The men of the houses where she worked would look at her with heightened interest. "Oho, hidden treasure." Mogri winked to herself as she hummed a Hindi film song, playing a game of titillation with the paunchy or suit-booted or balding homeowner who ogled her armpit, or her hips moving in the tightly bound cotton sari as she scrubbed the floors. Defeated and diminished, they looked to her like loyal animals standing up on their hind legs. This gave Mogri the courage and attitude with which she faced this world. In the bazaar she walked upright. She fought unabashedly with the shopkeepers. She stood outside the municipal toilet waiting her turn, with a tin of water in her hand, holding the same upright stance. Once in a while she even wondered whether she should go to Ratnagiri to see the stepmother and stepsiblings she had never seen.

Slowly, her friends scattered. Yamuna got a job as an ayah in a local hospital. When she left for the night shift, Mogri would walk with her to the bus stop. After dark, men would loiter around women who were alone at the bus stop. "Don't be afraid, Yamuna. We can rule the world if we keep the magic of our treasures hidden," Mogri would say, laughing loudly.

Yamuna did not quite understand this, but she laughed all the same, feeling a little afraid. But once the animals on their hind legs saw a woman laughing out loud, they retreated in despair.

The Shetty boy had already gone to Dubai, entrusting his shop to a man who had come from his home village. Occasionally, Mogri remembered those moments of pleasure she had with the Shetty boy in the unfinished building. But she would become indifferent, as though she could create those moments in herself at any time. There were no signs of Baba returning from Ratnagiri. Mogri decided to look for a job. In an alley next to the vegetable market, she saw the newly opened Sundar Bar with a board outside saying "Ladies Wanted," and went straight inside. It was a dingy room, like a matchbox, with lamps that seemed to throw darkness rather than light. There were longish seats, the smell of agarbattis mixed with cigarette smoke, and a ceiling so low that you could hit your head on it. Mogri felt like she had stepped into a luxury bus. In the bar, leaning against each seat, stood women like decorated dolls.

It took only a few minutes for Mogri to learn the work. One had to dress nicely and as fashionably as possible. When the women workers came in, the manager made them all stand in a line and sprayed perfume on their necks and saris. Laughing, they would smear it on their arms and bodies before going to their positions. When a customer came in, they had to smile. They had to bring the customer his drink from the counter. If it was beer, it had to be poured without spilling over. When Mogri poured beer for the first time without spilling a drop, the manager and the waiters were all impressed. These were the prescribed rules. After these, everything depended on individual talent. How to flirt with customers, how to pretend to be angry and say "Naughty, naughty." How to bend while pouring out the beer so that the jasmine flowers in her hair tickled the customer's nose. How to touch even while not touching, and move swiftly away. No limits to the games of the secret treasure. Very soon, Mogri became the queen of that game. Her skill left the other girls jealous. She began to get large tips. The manager who sat at the counter played umpire from a distance. He would indicate who was out, who was caught leg-before-wicket, who should be avoided, who should be left alone, and how the lords of the underworld should be treated. It took just a week for Mogri to master all this.

The men who bought vegetables at the market with serious faces. The men who dropped their uniformed children at school in their cars. The men who dressed up to go with their wives to weddings. All of them came into this bar surreptitiously, and came to get drunk. Mogri began to feel sorry for them. They waited in agony for her slightest touch. But if they saw her on the street, they would ignore her. If she smiled familiarly at them, they behaved as though they had stepped on a snake. Slowly, Mogri became the leader of the girls in the bar. She fought to have an autorickshaw to drop the girls—who went out with notes stuffed into their blouses—at their homes at night or at least at the nearest station. She began to learn the many facets of the game. There were married women there too, and ones with children. One of their husbands used to come to pick up his wife himself. They used to put their mangalsutras away and come to the bar with assumed names—Mona,

Reena, Rekha—so that they wouldn't be recognized. Girls from the western suburbs went to work in the eastern suburbs and the other way around. No one let on at home that they were working in a bar. The same women who walked upright on the street would shrink into themselves and perhaps use an umbrella for cover when they slipped into the bar, or they would come through the back door even if it meant walking through slush. This used to upset Mogri. "Let the customers slink in if they like," she argued, "but why should we come in like thieves?" The other women were irritated by her ideas. She told everyone that she worked in the bar, and swaggered down the street before entering through the main door. If customers asked her name, she would jokingly say "Why do you want to know my name?" but never lied to them. In her chawl, the girls who were waiting to get married began to avoid her. But all the uncles began to look at her in a new way. When her father came back from his Ratnagiri exile, he brought mangoes with him. When he heard that Baby was working in a bar, he was upset, but couldn't open his mouth in front of her. He took some of the mangoes to his other family in Jogeshwari. Only Mogri's mother knew that he had small children there. Mogri felt angry. Although she had accepted the woman in Ratnagiri as her father's first wife, it seemed far more difficult to accept the third one in Jogeshwari.

By and by, the bar began to attract a large number

of younger customers. The boys who used to hang around at the street corner began to come in with the rich Gujarati fellows. These rich boys came in chewing Pan Parag and holding videocassettes, while the chawl boys were in their rubber slippers, tucking the hair behind their ears, pulling their shirts down as they huddled into a corner. They would catch their reflections in a nearby mirror and get frightened. These were the same boys who had grown up in front of Mogri—Cycle Kaka's son, Yamuna's kid brother, the carrom-playing boy from the next building. To see that they had already joined the tribe of two-legged animals hurt her. One day she went into their houses and scolded all of them.

They yelled back at her, saying, "Get out, you! We know all about you. Are we drinking with your money, then?" Today they had deliberately come to the bar in a big group. They went up to the manager and said something. Then a fellow chewing his Pan Parag came up to Mogri, held her, shook her hard, shouting at her. Then her sari pallu fell. Blinking at her chest, the creature said "Wah" appreciatively. In a flash, Mogri had slapped him hard on the cheek. At that very second, she lost her job.

Staying at home, Mogri felt convinced that what she had done was right. *No one has the right to do anything to my body without my consent*, she thought, as she pounded her thigh with her fist. The boys did not appear in front of her now. Her friend Yamuna had taken up with a

young man in the hospital where she worked. "I'm getting married," she told Mogri.

"Whatever," said Mogri. "I'm not coming to Pearl
Centre with you again."

"Cheh, cheh," said Yamuna, "this is love."

Mogri guffawed. "Oh, then this is petty change
from that secret treasure." She thought pleasurably of
the Shetty boy, who had opened her secret treasure
without wasting words like *love*.

A number of families came to occupy the flats in
the building in which she and the boy used to go on
their treasure hunt. Everywhere you looked, there were
clothes drying, vessels being washed, the smell of cooking, women recovering from childbirth. In all the rooms
of all the houses were hidden—under the carpet—the
stolen pleasures of her friends and herself. *Why do these
people need so much space?* thought Mogri. Her own home
was so small. They had a wooden cupboard, some utensils, and a mattress—that was all. Perhaps these people
had a lot of things to hide. And who knows what they
hid in all those rooms. Her mother had stopped going
to work in those houses now.

One afternoon as she sat looking through the em-
ployment columns of the newspaper, she heard a huge
noise outside the building. People came running. The
Shah woman from the fifth floor had jumped. Her skull
was cracked. Until the Shiv Sena ambulance came, she
kept mumbling, "My husband, my husband." *This, too,*

must be a secret treasure problem, thought Mogri. She had seen for herself that the woman's husband, Shahbhai, was one of those two-legged animals. Stupid of the woman to try killing herself for that reason. And there was that colleague of hers from the bar who had an abortion when she was three months pregnant for fear of losing her job. All idiots.

Yamuna's wedding date got fixed. While discussing what kind of sari she should buy, embracing Mogri and wiping her eyes, Yamuna finally said, "Mogri, a request. Don't misunderstand me. I don't want you to come to the wedding."

Mogri was filled with anger, not sadness. "Your fate!" she exclaimed, as she bought a steel vessel as a wedding gift, and sent it to Yamuna without an inscription on it. Mogri's mother grumbled that she, too, should have found a nice "house."

"And what does that mean?" asked Mogri, as she rubbed her mother's feet with pain-relieving oil. Two trunks. One cupboard, one kerosene stove, a plastic wire to hang clothes on, a range of utensils nestling comfortably on three shelves each about two and a half feet long, a folded dhurrie, a vessel for drinking water, a bucket, a mirror hanging on a single nail, bangles hanging from that same nail, the bindis stuck on the mirror bottom. That was all. A home.

Now what had Yamuna done? She would go from just one such home to another exactly like it with pomp and ceremony. Like Dagadu from the chawl below them, maybe Yamuna's groom would also come riding on a horse. Wah! What an adventure for Yamuna. And in just such a tiny hut, in the shadows thrown by a kerosene lamp, he would ride her like a thief and then send her to her mother's for the delivery, with demands for a new steel balti, a new stove, and a piece of shirting. What great choice had Yamuna made?

Mogri had shouted and screamed when her father took two of her faded childhood frocks to Jogeshwari to his other family. When her mother said, "It's all right, the child's young," and packed the frocks herself, Mogri was stunned into silence. She thought of how her father, like the Shetty boy, was conducting his life quietly, without any fuss. Finally, she managed to get herself a job in the Light of India Irani restaurant at Flora Fountain, after begging everyone she knew to find her work.

Light of India was so different from Sunder Bar that Mogri felt as if she had been born again. It was so different from that hole in the wall bar near the vegetable market. Every day, the restaurant filled her with new breath. The small, round marble tables and the wooden chairs, the ancient, winged fans, the clean whitewashed walls, the three brothers who took turns at the cash counter and who carefully explained the tasks to Mogri in great detail. Keeping an account of how many soft drinks, breads, and eggs were consumed every day, checking the stocks in the kitchen, preparing bills, going to the bank from time to time, keeping track of staff salaries and leaves taken, Mogri became the assistant to the aging owners. Her last task of the day was to wind the old clock with its Roman numerals.

In the kitchen, Thambi and Badebhai, both past forty, still engaged in constant banter, keeping everyone's spirits high.

"Badebhai should have been working at the Taj Mahal Hotel. By mistake he's ended up here, making omelettes," Thambi would say.

"Thambi fell into a barrel of tar one day. That's why he's this color," Badebhai would needle him.

When their taunts got too loud, the owner would shout at them. When the scolding was too harsh, the cooks would puff out their faces. Badebhai would sing "Yeh Hai Bombay Meri Jaan." Thambi's omelettes fluffed up nicely. Even when he revealed his secret formula—adding a bit of water while beating the egg—Badebhai's omelettes always came out flat. So it was Thambi who always ended up making them. Mogri would go into the kitchen once in a while to hurry them up.

The three waiter kakas were well past fifty, and Mogri used to feel bad seeing these old men working in a restaurant. In their white cotton pants and coat uniform, they looked like railway ticket collectors. They moved with ease around the restaurant, wiping down a table as soon as the customers had left. When there were no customers, the waiters stood like silent pillars in a corner. When Mogri first came to work there, the three waiters seemed a little irritated, but they soon responded to her simple ways and became quite friendly.

Once, the restaurant used to serve only biscuits, cakes, omelettes, and tea. But since this did not make ends meet, they had also started serving beer some years ago. In the airy atmosphere of Light of India, the same beer bottles that looked like terrifying objects in Sunder Bar were filled with sparkling yellow liquid. Mogri's eye gladdened at the sight of a mug filled with beer. Before Mogri had come to the restaurant, it had always been one of the waiters who opened the beer bottle for a customer. Now that task fell to Mogri. If one of the kakas was on leave, she took the order herself. The younger brother who sat behind the counter used to keep the top button of his shirt open, but after Mogri arrived, he began to fasten it. In the four hundred square feet of Light of India, the light played hide and seek. The knots in Mogri's mind loosened. She felt her anxieties melting away in spite of not talking to anybody about them.

Soon after she joined, the three kakas began to speak to her. She didn't understand what explanations lay behind some of the details they shared. She didn't know where they lived, what they did with their salaries. But if Mogri didn't come to work, they all missed her. If she patted one of them even slightly on the back, the waiter's eyes sparkled. These old men, who probably slept under a ladder or a cot somewhere in the armpit of this inhuman city, waited every morning to see Mogri's happy and healthy face. Before starting work they all drank a cup of strong chai together, and then started wiping the tables with the enthusiasm of small children.

The people who came to the restaurant seemed to be there for the open air and the light. Some would sit for hours, with a bottle of beer and a book. Sometimes friends, and lovers, would sit there in silence, also for a long time, sipping endless cups of tea. Mogri felt fondly toward the friends who sat without speaking, merely spending time with each other. Those waiting for a lover, those tired after a shopping expedition, those on their way to their cavelike homes after having left their cavelike offices—they were all here for the calm light and the airy space of the restaurant. How gentle these desires were, she felt. Even the jeans-clad Malayali boys with their curly hair, selling electronic goods in their little booths outside, looked different when they came alone into the restaurant for a cup of tea. There was a sort of peace here beyond the bustle of the street, so much so that the few who came in intent on making a racket were taken aback at the quiet atmosphere and left as quickly as they could, to look for another restaurant.

The moment Mogri stepped inside the restaurant, her chawl, her mother, Yamuna, the dirty vessels to be washed in people's homes, the sweaty two-legged animals seemed to recede far away. Until she went home in the crowded train compartment, she didn't remember a thing. Instead, she cherished the special moments of the day and was glad. The students of the nearby art school used to come to Light of India for tea. The moment she saw a beard and a cloth bag and a crooked smile, she knew this was an artist. If any of them came in wearing dirty clothes, Mogri and the oldest waiter felt irritated. Some sat in the restaurant and sketched the scenes outside. If someone was around to listen to them, the artists held forth with big words. Mogri used to wonder why even the best sketchers spoke so much. So as not to ruin their folders by carrying them in the crowded train, some students used to leave them in the café. Once she saw the old waiter looking into the folders with great interest.

She found out that the old kaka used to draw publicity posters for Prabhat Theatres once upon a time. Then he became a pimp in Kamathipura, where he married one of the girls, who left him in due course. Mogri came to know these things in bits and pieces from the others in the restaurant. This kaka was also the one who always painted the restaurant walls. This time around, he applied whitewash on the walls as well as the pillars, both wooden and concrete, establishing in the eyes of everyone that both kinds were permanent. He was the waiter who spoke with more English words than the others. He always said to Mogri, "Take care, take care." When Thambi told her that the kaka had plied his trade with thousands of young girls, Mogri felt strange. She also heard that he used to tell stories that would arouse young men: what Nepali women are like; why there was so much demand for them; how young virgins were "inaugurated"; how to know if a woman had a disease; when to eat a palang-tod paan. Even now he would go over these stories with an old soldier's enthusiasm, in front of Mogri, too. Wearing his patched white cotton jacket, the waiter would wink as he said in English: "I am retired now. Retired hurt." Once he so completely forgot himself that he pinched Mogri on the chin, saying, "So tender! Too late. You should have come to me at sixteen. I would have made you a queen, a queen!" Immediately after, he wept loudly, his thin hand shaking, muttering, "Sorry, sorry." It was Mogri then who stroked his back affectionately and calmed him down.

Around this time, Mogri's father gave up his chowkidar job and sat at home. Mogri did not feel like saying anything. Her father and the Light of India kaka seemed the same to her now. She felt that their fatigue was identical. "What did you get out of setting up three families? Finally you have to live off my baby," taunted Mogri's mother. Annoyed, her father set off for Jogeshwari. He did not come back again. Maa used to keep a few chapatis and some rice for him every night, and then eat them herself the next day.

One day Mogri heard that Yamuna was having trouble with her delivery. She rushed to the hospital instead of going to work. There was no one from Yamuna's husband's family. Her mother and elder brother grabbed Mogri's hand and started weeping. Yamuna's condition was serious. When the doctor said it would be difficult to save the child, no one had the courage to tell him to save Yamuna first. So Mogri took that task upon herself. Then Yamuna was taken into the operating theater, and after a cesarean, she began to show signs of life but the infant could not be saved. Yamuna now held Mogri's hand, crying: "My child, my child! They killed my child." Mogri was unwillingly reminded of Yamuna's abortion at the Pearl Centre. She wondered where the Shetty boy was, who had given her eighty rupees for the abortion. "My husband won't take me back," wailed Yamuna. "Please get me a job. Even the bar will do."

The next day Mogri felt like telling the old kaka everything about the Shetty boy's antics. She also told him about her father's multiple families, and about the two-legged animals who tried to molest her from behind while she was washing their clothes in the bathroom. Smiling gently as though he knew it all, the kaka said, "Come with me this evening. Come and see where I live."

That afternoon it poured in the Flora Fountain area. Standing inside the restaurant, Mogri and the three waiters looked out at the rain beating down. "Idiots, you like looking at those art school children's silly sketches?

Here, imagine that the open door is a painting. Then see what an incredible scene lies in front of you."

Mogri, who was staring at the door, felt as though she had been struck by lightning. The door did indeed look like a frame, and the colors mingled outside in astonishing combinations. At the upper edge of the frame was the green of the shoots on the tree, glistening wet in the rain; lower down were the balls and balloons sold at the footpath shop; the yellow-topped taxis that kept driving past; many-hued umbrellas; people's wet clothes as they hurried by; a double-decker bus that suddenly painted the whole frame red. The kaka's idea of the painting had so gripped Mogri that she began to see each window of Light of India as a living picture. As she sat watching the open door, she was startled when some customers came in through it, taking off their raincoats and furling their umbrellas.

That evening Mogri set out with the old kaka. His aged body swayed as he walked. He had taken off the white uniform and put on a pair of black pants and a striped blue shirt. He stopped on the way to buy a packet of biscuits. When they got off the bus, it was on a street with colored lights. On either side were three-story buildings with cages where women wearing skimpy blouses and short petticoats were calling out to customers. They chewed on betel nut as they made lewd gestures to the passersby. In front of each cage was a man waiting to strike a bargain. When a customer entered the cage and sat down on a rickety cot, the chosen woman quickly drew a curtain and disappeared behind it with him. Mogri felt numb. The kaka said, "Don't be afraid. There's no one as sinless and helpless as these people. Remember the secret treasure you talked about? Do you know what their share is? Perhaps five rupees per customer. And several times a night."

Walking beside a run-down old shop and in between two cages, the kaka went ahead. Without being aware of it, Mogri had clutched his hand. On both sides, women were laughing loudly. They stroked Mogri and whistled. "Chacha ne aurat laaya, Chacha ne aurat laaya—Uncle's brought a woman," they said, pounding on the kaka's head.

"Nahi re, woh meri poti hai, she's my granddaughter," said the kaka, also in a teasing voice.

When he opened a small wooden door and went inside, Mogri saw that it was a room of about ten feet square. Two metal trunks, a green plastic bucket, a kerosene stove, two pairs of pants, and two shirts hanging on a peg. To one side a woman was sleeping with a sheet covering her. "This is Susheela," said the kaka. "From the neighboring kothi. She's pregnant. Right now is when the 'business' begins over there. So she comes here to sleep. I don't mind. If her back aches, I massage it for her. Her mother was a young girl when I was in the business."

Just then, Susheela turned over in her sleep. Mogri

could see her fair Nepali face, which was slightly swollen. Mogri was reminded of Yamuna. "And how is this painting?" asked the kaka. Outside the door of the cubbyhole, Mogri could see a row of lights. The kaka opened one of his trunks and showed her some brushes wrapped in paper and tied with a rubber band. "See, these are from my poster-painting days at Prabhat Studio." He put them back in the trunk. "Will you have some biscuits?" he asked.

Mogri felt something stirring inside her. A fat woman came in and checked Susheela's temperature by touching her hand. "Chacha, have you given your guest some tea?" she asked.

"No, Chaandi, I haven't made any yet. Aren't you well today?"

"My turn hasn't come yet, Chacha. Only after midnight. I'm getting old, that's why."

"Cheh, your lovely smile doesn't age," said the kaka, and was thumped on the head in return.

Laughing at the kaka, and lightly stroking Mogri as she passed, Chaandi left.

The kaka patted the mute Mogri's hand. "See, child, this is my family. Now you're part of it too," he said, laughing heartily. As the kaka and Mogri left, all the women called out to the girl: "Phir aana, come again."

Feeling strangely drawn to these women, Mogri went up to a few of them and shook hands as she said goodbye.

Kaka went with her in the bus to the train station. "Sorry for troubling you. You don't have to come here again," he said.

"No, Kaka," she began, but did not know what else to say. She had to run to catch the nine p.m. local.

Mogri clung to a pole awkwardly in the crowded compartment, her eyes filled with the light of the kaka's world. What free and easy relationships there were in his empire! These women clutching their bags and purses in the ladies', the heaps of hanging men hugging each other willy-nilly in the general compartment next door, the wire mesh between the two compartments and the countless eyes looking at the women hungrily through the mesh. It seemed as though a single creature with many eyes stood there. Outside rows and rows of houses were going past. A flash of a tiny home seen from the train—curtains, vessels, families that cooked a meal and rolled out the mattress just for their own members. When the train stopped at each station, an enormous flood of people poured in and out of the train. When Mogri started walking toward her chawl from Mulund Station, she felt stifled. She remembered the Nepali girl Susheela lying down under her Sholapur bedsheet.

As she entered the chawl, she heard a loud cry. Scared, she walked faster. Her mother was clinging to the water drum and crying loudly as she beat her chest. The women of the chawl were standing around her, but at a safe distance. They stepped back when they saw Mogri, who kneeled down beside her mother.

"What happened, Maa?" she asked.

"Your father—he had a stroke on his mistress's bed," said her mother, wailing again.

"How did you find out?" Mogri asked.

One of the women from the chawl said a man had come from Jogeshwari with the news, and had even left behind an address.

"He left such a lovely family and went after that whore. And to think he's fallen down on her bed." Maa went on crying.

Mogri was more upset at the way her mother was crying than at the news about her father's stroke. In the woman's wails, the word *bed* kept coming up again and again. Anywhere else would have been fine, but to have a stroke on "her" bed! Maa was trembling with anger. But neither she nor Mogri could think of what to do. When the crowd scattered, the two lay down to sleep. Mogri opened the biscuit packet the kaka had given her, and both of them ate the biscuits as they lay in bed. The door was open like the kaka's painting. Outside was a morbid mixture of light and darkness. Mogri's ears filled with the sweet, uninhibited chatter of the kaka's girls.

As soon as they woke the next morning, Mogri's mother said she would go to see "him."

"Yes, let's go together," said Mogri.

"No, no, let me go alone. You can go some other time. Write a letter to Ratnagiri. Don't tell them where it happened."

Both of them left the house together, and had a cup of tea near the station. Mogri went with her mother as far as Dadar, and put her on the train to Jogeshwari after explaining how she was to get to the address they had been given.

"I'll come in the evening. Stay there until then if you can." Marveling how her slender mother managed to get inside the crowded compartment, Mogri caught her train to Victoria Terminus.

Until she reached Light of India, Mogri's eyes were filled with the image of her maa, who had gone to see her husband, who lay paralyzed in his mistress's house. She wondered if her little stepsister was frightened about what had happened. When she reached the restaurant it was raining lightly in spite of the sunshine. The kaka was looking out for her anxiously, since she was late. His eyes widened, and he smiled when she came in. Mogri put her handbag down on the counter and set about her work. When the kaka came near, she asked him how Susheela was. As if to say she was fine, the kaka inclined his head, smiled, and patted Mogri's hand. Calmly, they stood together, looking at the incandescent door.

"Mogriya Satsanga," 1991

A TRUCK FULL OF CHRYSANTHEMUMS

A WINDOW IN THE LAST KHOLI OF THE MUNICIPAL CHAWL IS always open. Seen from the street, the open window looks like a blind man's eye. Covered with a Sholapur chadar that smells of Amrutanjan, Durgi lies with her eyes open, her small arms and legs making her look like a child in spite of her sixty years.

The discarded dresses of the girls of the house, who have grown quite big, now clothe Durgi. Even those sit loosely on her. However weak she feels, Durgi crawls to the window on her stomach and looks out. When she sees a new day spreading itself out on the street, she opens her eyes as though a flower of gratitude has bloomed. She looks down at the children going to school, without the strength to call out to them. Her belongings—the old cup, the plastic mug, the comb with its big

teeth, the palm-size plastic mirror—sit near her mat. A strange
silence seems to surround this mat.

Sudhir Mahajan worked in a municipal office. His
wife, Jyoti, on the strength of a long-ago college education, gave after-school lessons at home. The two
children, Rashmi and Varsha, were growing up rapidly.
Both had the mother's attitude and the father's walk.
When the elder one, Rashmi, was an infant, Durgi
came into this one-room envelope of a house to look
after the baby and do the housework in exchange for
two meals a day, a sari once a year, and the promise of
a separate bank account "in which we will put your
salary." When Rashmi was three years old, Varsha was
born. By the time the baby woke up and needed to be
fed, the older sister had to be made ready for school.
By the time Durgi plaited the girl's hair, it was time to
wash the clothes and scrub the vessels before the water supply stopped for the day. Just as all the household
chores were done, it was time to go and stand in the
ration queue. Since there were so many things to take
care of, the Mahajan family did not think of throwing
Durgi out, and thus twenty years passed. By the time
the girls' dupattas were to be found lying everywhere
in the house, and they had gone through college, Durgi
had become an inseparable part of the family, like the
worn iron handle of the metal cupboard, and like the
faded embroidered cloth over the TV set. "She's of
some help to us, and who else does she have?" With this

wobbly logic, Mahajan stopped putting money into her account. After dinner, on the rare occasion when there was an apple being eaten, the fact that Durgi always got a small slice was a matter of great pride for the Mahajan family.

For the grown-up children, however, Durgi's presence was like an obstacle. *Where has my hair clip disappeared to?* they would rage. When Durgi sat down to supper after they had all eaten, the girls would start taking out their homework as though to hasten her. In that small space, there was no question of all of them sleeping with their limbs stretched out. Especially after the girls had grown so tall. They all felt as though they were sleeping standing up, like in the local train.

It was during Rashmi's tenth-grade exams that the symptoms of Durgi's illness first began to seem serious. She kept getting a fever. Without sending her to a doctor, the Mahajans treated her with balms and aspirin. Since Rashmi had to study late, it was almost impossible for Durgi to sleep whenever she wanted. Her face and limbs began to swell. A hundred aches and pains exhausted her. "You take it easy, Durgi. Don't put your hands in water. It's not good for you," Mrs. Mahajan would say. But since she never got up to do a task, Durgi would end up dealing with the chores. Then Mrs. Mahajan would pretend to be angry. One day, unable to contain herself until she could reach the mori, Durgi puked all over the house, and on the people around.

Then she began to wipe the vomit desperately with her weak hands from a thigh here and an arm there. The crack that existed between her and the others revealed itself in that awful silence. They all sat unmoving while Durgi tried to clean up the mess from their clothes. From that day onward, the smell of vomit lingered permanently in the house.

"All this happened because we've let her stay here. Let's at least send her away now," whispered Sudhir Mahajan.

"What will the neighbors say? That we threw her out after all these years when she fell ill? Let's take her to the doctor and then send her off," said the wife.

As though possessed, Mahajan dragged Durgi to three different doctors. But it didn't look like the sickness was going to end soon. Seeing the blood test reports, one of the doctors began to speak gravely of big treatments in big hospitals. Mahajan's limbs began to shiver. He never took his wife and children to doctors for fear of the expense. So he came home with a few lies: taking some vitamins will do the trick, maybe a change of climate would work. He spoke without looking his wife in the eye. Mrs. Mahajan remembered the days when Durgi, upset at some small thing, would say she was leaving, and her employer would cajole her back, saying she was like her elder sister, and that they would look after her.

"But is she your real sister? Is she a blood relation?

If you pay a salary, anyone will work for you. There's a limit to how much we can do," said Mahajan, drawing his wife outside.

"But Durgi looked after our girls without neglecting them. During your strike, for months she lied to us that her stomach was upset, and ate only a small meal once a day. We can't forget all these things," said the wife.

After this discussion, both of them would come back with fresh enthusiasm and put up with Durgi for a while longer. "Let me know if you want to go to your native place, or to your relatives. I can take you there. Try to remember, do you have any relatives?" coaxed Mahajan. But Durgi only stared blankly at him. Even during daylight hours, Durgi's tattered mat was always spread out, and seemed to make the silence harsh and noisy.

The students began to avoid coming for their lessons. Rashmi and Varsha began to kick up a row over the smallest matter, and sometimes would get up and leave in the middle of dinner. They said their friends didn't want to visit them at home. The chawl people began to say Durgi's sickness was infectious. But they would come to borrow some onions or a matchbox, and say how good the Mahajans were, how nicely they were looking after their sick servant without sending her away. Now Durgi could not stand up by herself. She had to be led by hand to the toilet. She had fallen down while coming back from the chawl's common bathrooms, and it needed several people to lift her and bring her back. After this she took to her bed permanently. Mahajan sat with his hand on his head. It was clear that Durgi would not now leave the house alive. Even if she called out from her bed, they pretended not to hear. The couple had been saving every paisa for the weddings of their daughters, and did not dare think of a hospital for Durgi. And the neighbors kept saying so that Durgi could also hear: "How good you people are. Even her family would not have looked after her like this."

Mrs. Mahajan could not stomach having to help Durgi with her ablutions. Durgi, who could have died of embarrassment for causing trouble, stopped eating altogether. Only when her mouth dried did Durgi sprinkle a few drops on it. Mahajan's blood pressure started rising. His daughters, instead of sparkling, were looking like the windows of bankrupt shops.

"Now people will start coming home to see the girls. How can we have them in here?" Mrs. Mahajan began to cry out loud in the neighbors' houses.

Some said to her: "Stop giving her food and water."

"Cheh, cheh," she would respond, but on coming home she would peer into the water tumbler by the mat to see how much was remaining. It was still full.

"Why don't you drink the water?" Mrs. Mahajan would shriek tearfully.

Like a frightened sparrow, when Durgi put out

her shaking hands toward the tumbler, Mrs. Mahajan screamed, "Don't drink it if you don't want to. Don't do me any favors!" And Durgi would draw her hand back inside her sheet.

Mahajan spoke to his well-wishers at his office. On someone's suggestion, he went to a doctor in an old lane of the suburb. The doctor welcomed him silently. In a low voice, he asked for details of Mahajan's problem. Then he took a large amount of money as his fee, and said: "My name cannot be mentioned anywhere, mister. Give her these ten pills before she sleeps. Let her swallow them herself. You may go now."

Trembling, Mahajan walked back through the lane.

Although it had been nearly a month since Durgi stopped eating and drinking, her life still burned bright. Her eyes looked deeply into things. Like an animal, she would drag herself, stomach on the floor, toward the window, where she would cling to the bars. Outside on the street was a wholesale distribution center for fruit, vegetables, and flowers, where trucks came from all corners and emptied themselves. Years ago, she herself had come in one such truck, having begged a ride from its driver. She wondered where that truck was now. The incense burning on its dashboard still lingered in her nostrils. So many kinds of trucks, carrying watermelon, cabbage, cauliflower, orange. As she gazed, her sight grew dim and she leaned on the window bars. When she opened her eyes again, the trucks stood empty. But the truck full of chrysanthemums in the corner stood as it was. She gazed until her eyes dimmed again, and then dragged herself back to her mat. In her eyes, the truck full of chrysanthemums kept standing there without ever getting empty.

That night the Mahajans sent their daughters out of the room, and after bolting the door, they came and sat with their heads bowed in front of Durgi.

Mahajan began to say "Durgi . . ." and could not finish his sentence.

"Rashmi, Varsha, to be married . . . society . . ." stammered Mrs. Mahajan, her throat dry.

As though she understood everything, Durgi waved a trembling hand at her and then put her hand out obediently.

As though sleepwalking, Mahajan reached out for his office bag, took out the packet of pills with a shaking hand, and gave it to Durgi. She seemed to be struggling to say something. Mrs. Mahajan bent down and put her ear close to Durgi's mouth. "I'll take them . . . but tomorrow . . . I'll take them tomorrow," whispered Durgi.

As though all this did not concern them at all, the Mahajans rushed out of the room and started walking in the street. If they stopped, they seemed to hear Durgi's helpless plea: "Tomorrow . . ."

Let her be today, they thought.

When they came back to the chawl, Rashmi and

Varsha were already eating their dinner. They had the TV on full blast. The husband and wife did not have the courage to look in Durgi's direction. Mrs. Mahajan changed the water in the tumbler next to Durgi's mat. She went to plait Durgi's hair, which she did once a week after oiling it, and Durgi refused, pressing her head tight against the window. But afterward, she called Varsha and Rashmi and insisted that they should be the ones plaiting her hair.

Afraid of the fiery look their mother gave them, the girls quickly put some oil on Durgi's thin hair and then braided it. As she shook her head while it was being oiled, the reflections of the tube lights in the room trembled like silver lamps in Durgi's eyes. Then Durgi spoke with great effort about a long-forgotten birthday of the infant Varsha when she had piddled in front of all the guests. She asked them to hold a mirror in front of her, and gazed into it as though looking at a picture. She then signaled to everyone to turn out the lights and go to sleep, and dragged herself to the window. Rashmi and Varsha fought with each other as usual over the bedsheets. The Mahajan couple sat sleeplessly at the entrance to the room.

As the night wore on, there were fewer and fewer people in the street below, and one could see it quite empty in the distance. The empty trucks were hiding here and there. Except for the truck full of chrysanthemums, the rest of the fruit market looked like a piece of wastepaper. Soon someone would open the back of this truck and start shoveling the flowers into the street. This longest night of the century was holding off tomorrow with all its might.

"Sevanthi Hoovina Trakku," 1997

TICK TICK FRIEND

Nanavati Hospital in Vile Parle West has recently set up a television studio in the basement of the building in front of the main hospital. Different television channels use this studio to shoot their quizzes and song contests. So in the hospital environs, one sees a peculiar mix of people: the patients and their relatives along with the young quiz contestants and their ambitious parents. The parents of the contestants are sometimes taken aback by the wheelchairs, the lines for the Outpatient department, and the hordes of patients inside; but the patients sometimes get enthused by the contestants and their minders, who in a show of sheepish pride caress their bright-eyed, neatly combed children from time to time.

"Who is the American president who cultivated peanuts?"

"In which sport is the term *Chinaman* used?"

Forgetting the answers occasionally, the children go through general-knowledge books in helpless last-minute concentration, disturbed only by the ambulances that come in with their sirens screaming. The children watch with fearful eyes as a patient is brought out of one such ambulance and taken away into Emergency, looking fragile on the stretcher.

"Don't look there," say the parents.

"Do you want some chips?" ask anxious fathers.

At least four or five episodes are shot every day. The cameramen and assistant directors who come out to smoke mingle with the white-coated young doctors and the nurses on their rounds.

When Madhubani came running into the hospital compound to join the throng, her father, Sohanlal, was left behind, unable to walk any faster. They had arrived just that morning at Dadar Station from Bhusawal, and had paid to get into the waiting room to finish a hurried wash, got into the local train asking for Nanavati Hospital, gotten off at Vile Parle Station, and had been told by a tea vendor that the hospital was only ten minutes away, and then hurried to the quiz venue. As soon as he said "Nanavati Hospital" on the train, someone had asked, "Arre, who's sick?"

Sohanlal had immediately responded, "No, no! It's the zonal-level TV quiz contest—my daughter's very clever; she's already at the Taluk level; she . . ." Before he could finish his sentence, the train stopped at a station, and people began to push the father and daughter aside, "Get down . . . don't stand in the way."

Screeching and pushing, the people who had surrounded them were now replaced by a new bunch of people, with new noses, new brows, and new eyes.

Approaching the hospital on foot, Madhubani broke into a run, saying, "We're getting late!"

Clutching their blue suitcase, Sohanlal shouted to her to go slow, and fell back as she ran ahead, moving as if in slow motion. Keeping his eyes on his daughter, he said, "Go get your name registered!"

Having given her name, Madhubani came out again, and seeing her father sitting on top of the suitcase on the footpath mopping his neck with a kerchief, she signaled to him that there was time, and he shouldn't worry.

"If we have time, you should get something to eat. You haven't had anything this morning, Madhu," said Sohanlal. Both of them walked slowly to the hospital canteen.

Hospital canteens have a uniquely mellow atmosphere. The kind of greedy anticipation found in regular restaurants and canteens, the subconscious smile with which an expectant customer greets the waiter bearing a tray on which rests a dosa or a large puri—you didn't see that here. What you saw were people filling thermoses for the patients under their care, grabbing a quick bite while wondering anxiously whether the duty doctor might come around when they were away in the canteen.

Madhubani ordered a dosa. At the table across from her was a good-looking young man who seemed to have been sitting there for some time.

"Is it good?" he asked her.

For a while she could not figure out what he was referring to. Then she understood and said, "Yes, it's good."

"Then I'll have one too," he said, calling the waiter.

The young man turned to them and asked: "Quiz?" His shining eyes seemed to dull a little when they stretched while asking a question. His easy posture suggested that he had been in the hospital environment for a long time. "Who's your guest on the quiz today? I heard that yesterday Shah Rukh Khan had come. The kids in our ward were talking about him. There was a rumor that he'd come into the children's wards, but the poor things waited in vain all day." Then, as if wondering whether his listeners were getting tired of his quick speech, the man changed his tone a little: "What's the prize? A trip to the Taj Mahal or pounds of chocolate?"

Sohanlal suddenly said: "Will they give us cash instead of the prize if we ask them?"

The young man pointed to the board behind the canteen payment counter that read in English, "No Credit, Only Cash," and said, "Oh, you're taking that board very seriously!" He started laughing. Madhubani knew that her father would not like this. Perhaps at another time and in another place she, too, would have been irritated. But because of his hospital gown, the young man's behavior appeared both simple and tolerable.

"Now you have to answer my quiz. You'll have four options. Don't be afraid. The first question: What is my name? Answers to choose from: A. Santanam, B. Joy, C. Buddhooram, D. Makarand. Come on! Your time starts now. Don't think too much about it. Just tell me the answer . . ." He started making the tick-tick-tick sound of a clock.

Madhubani began to think in earnest. She began to compare the names with what she perceived as the man's nature. She was in the tenth grade. The man was probably about ten years older than her. This sharp-looking man could not possibly be called Buddhooram! With his sparkling eyes and long fingers, the name Santanam didn't suit. (*Hurry up—your time is nearly up!*) Joy somehow sounded either like the name of an ice cream or a tailor shop. This person, eating his dosa rather delicately in his blue uniform, had to be called Makarand. So she said, "Option D. Makarand."

"Oh no! Sorry, my name is Buddhooram. Truly," said the young man.

Sohanlal got up hurriedly. Madhubani said with some disappointment, "Your name can't be Buddhooram."

"Why not? People call me Buddhoo affectionately. Don't you like it?"

The man reached out to pick up a white paper napkin from the table, made a tiny boat out of it, and handed it to Madhubani. "Enjoy your quiz. Quiz questions are to be enjoyed. You see that hospital board there, saying 'Inquiry'? No one can enjoy any question that's asked there. But a quiz is different. It's like asking in this canteen, 'What's there to eat?' You don't have to know the answer to enjoy the question. Who knows? By the time you arrive at the answer, the fun would have gone out of it.

"Okay, I have a request: if Kareena Kapoor comes to your quiz as a guest, please get her autograph for me on this paper boat. I'm crazy about her. She hides the entire universe's moonlight inside her. That's why there's so much darkness around us. But if she smiles . . . wah! Please dear, get her autograph for me . . ."

The young man took the bill out of Sohanlal's hand and said, "Please don't say no. This is on me, with my best wishes."

As though accepting the hospitality unwillingly, Sohanlal said, "Thanks. I hope you get well soon."

The man shook his hand. Then he stroked Madhubani's head along the parting and said, "If they ask you what disease wipes away one's memories, the answer is Alzheimer's."

By the time she reached the studio with her father, Madhubani's mind felt cleansed. Who was this Buddhooram? She felt she had just been born, sitting in front of that man, eating her dosa at the canteen table. How immersed he was in what he said!

Sohanlal said, "Poor man . . . he must be very intelligent . . . see how he's been struck by disease at such a young age. What did he say it was called? Do you remember? Perhaps you'll get a question on it."

Madhubani felt bad that they had both assumed the young man had this disease when all he had been doing was perhaps giving them information about it. Buddhooram's hair was very short. Was that because of the style he had adopted, or because of the medicines he was taking? His face seemed brighter because of the short hair.

The studio was boiling over. The parents in the audience were being ordered about, and arranged according to their height and color of clothing. "You in the blue shirt, go and sit over there. You, yellow dupatta, come this side."

Each parent was focusing on the child they had escorted. Madhubani felt her wits desert her under the scorching lights. Buddhooram was right. The entire world was in darkness. All that she had mugged up in the last five months for the quiz—the height of the pyramids, the seals of Mohenjodaro, the weight of the atom bomb that had fallen on Nagasaki—all these were in darkness. The golden girl Kareena Kapoor needed to come here and smile, to scatter her moonlight and save everyone from darkness. Buddhooram hadn't even asked their names, mused Madhubani. A woman in tight jeans came to the stage and started reading out the regulations. Parents started twitching in their seats, giving a thumbs-up sign, or raising a fist, or using other awkward signs to encourage their ward. Since there was a bright light next to Sohanlal, Madhubani couldn't see his face clearly. There were a couple of giant screens in the room, on which everyone's face could be seen now and then. Madhubani had chosen her best clothes, starched and ironed them, and put them on in the dirty waiting room at Dadar Station. But the journey in the local train had seriously creased her dress, and she felt that everyone else was sparkling in unwrinkled clothes in contrast. But everyone's face had a sort of fearful, nonhuman smile, as though to say "thus far and no farther."

Madhubani felt like going back to the canteen. In the midst of such pain and suffering and terror, the hospital canteen had seemed such a comforting place. Even the waiters there seemed to have the qualities of a nurse. The sweets in the glass cupboard at the counter didn't seem incongruous at all. With the awareness of widespread suffering, private hunger and thirst was dealt with in a subdued way in that place. Shouldn't the world be like that too?

All the lights were now on. In contrast, the areas that were unlit looked even darker. From the dark sea in front came the sound of clapping, wave after wave. The quizmaster, clad in a colorful coat, spoke in spurts with feigned enthusiasm. When he heard Madhubani's name, he said, "What a beautiful name! Can you tell me what this name is famous for?"

She felt embarrassed to speak about her own name, and debated whether to say anything or not. The candidates on either side of her raised their hands.

"It's a form of folk art!"

"Tribal art," they said, to thunderous clapping from the audience.

Madhubani felt like laughing.

Sohanlal was upset that his foolish daughter had not spoken up, even though she knew the answer. It was useless to have bought her a secondhand bicycle when she had entered the tenth grade, he thought.

As Madhubani began to wonder what the quizmaster would have done with Buddhooram's name if he had been a candidate, the questions started. The sound of the buzzer, the marks going up, the right answer, the wrong answer. *Is that a guess? Is it right? Your time begins now . . . tick . . . tick . . . tick . . .*

The quizmaster spoke English in such a convoluted way that Madhubani's ears buzzed. But she was doing well. Then the quizmaster asked: "Madhubani, a special question for you. The Bhopal gas tragedy—in which four thousand people perished—on which date did it happen? It took place after midnight. You don't have to tell me the time, just the date.

"Your time begins now. A. September 16, B. August . . ."

Madhubani felt dizzy. She remembered the tragedy—that poison-filled night, the deep silence. Their neighbor Jyotsna Bhabhi and her daughter Sejal were to arrive in Bhopal that night. But the train had passed through the fog of poison, and stood at the station filled with corpses. Those who were running collapsed even as they ran. Those who were alighting from the train fell as they got down. The entire world had fallen silent when the bodies of Jyotsna Bhabhi and the eight-year-old Sejal, wrapped in white cloth, were lifted out of the green tempo. Within seconds the silence was riven by Bhavesh Bhai's scream as he stroked his wife's forehead, nose, and face through the white sheet with trembling fingers. And then they had to tear Sejal's body away from his lap. Bhavesh Bhai had lifted both his hands to the skies and howled . . .

"Lights off!"

"Bring some water here . . ."

"Let in some air . . ."

Madhubani opened her eyes to find herself lying on the sofa in the makeup room. Sohanlal asked her if she wanted some coffee.

"Cheh, if you had answered this one question you would have won. How many times have I told you to eat properly? How could you forget the day that Jyotsna Bhabhi died?" he said helplessly.

"Jyotsna   Bhabhi . . . Sejal—" said Madhubani through lips that had gone white, as she began to sob.

"Six years since they left us," said Sohanlal. "I was the one who took Bhavesh Bhai by the hand and wandered in the hot sun through Gwalior, Jabalpur, and Jhansi seeking compensation. I spent my own money doing this . . . People said I was trying to hoodwink Bhavesh Bhai and grab half the money. He, too, began to believe it. Then he went off on his own, and after six years he's still trying to get his relief. I'm the one who should cry, not you. You don't know what humiliation is. You'd come to the final point. You'd have won this contest . . ." There was no gap between his sorrow and his rage.

The quizmaster had come in to change his coat, and Sohanlal said to him, "Please give her another chance. We didn't sleep much on the train coming here. And she didn't eat properly this morning. That's why she felt weak. Please, sir. We've come with a lot of hope. If she wins this prize, her future education will be taken care of. I want her to do well in life. She's a very clever girl . . . but . . ."

Madhubani squirmed to see her father grovel. He went on: "People very close to us died in the Bhopal gas tragedy. Our neighbors. Their dead bodies were brought into our own yard. She's very sensitive. The moment you said 'gas tragedy,' she remembered all that and went blank. She knows that date very well."

Madhubani covered her face with her hands.

"Okay, let's see," said the quizmaster. "If a candidate

fails to show up for the afternoon episode, we can take her. Your daughter's a smart girl. But if she had given this answer and then fainted, she would have been seen as a brave heroine." Laughing a strange laugh meant to win everyone over, the man walked out of the room.

Looking back at his daughter, Sohanlal ran after him.

A strong spotlight from the set was reflected in the mirrors of the makeup room. Along with two of the contestants, their mothers, too, were changing their clothes. The bulbs in the bracket above shone brightly on the wall of mirrors.

After Jyotsna Bhabhi and Sejal had died, Bhavesh Bhai used to eat his meals in their house. One day during the meal, Sohanlal had said, "Either you should believe in me completely, or not at all. There's no such thing as half-half in trust. Or in honesty. Trust me, or don't trust me—that's all."

After this, Bhavesh Bhai had slowly stopped coming to eat with them. Someone told them that he was now sleeping on the veranda of a city lawyer's house to make it easier to go to court regularly. From time to time, Madhubani used to be consumed by that silence that couldn't be shattered, the silence in which the two white-sheeted bodies, one big and one small, were brought down from the green tempo. She could will herself to go into that silence at any time. Once she had gone looking for a lost ball in the deserted field behind her school, and there in the unfamiliar green bushes she had suddenly seen a hundred strange yellow flowers. On that occasion, too, the deep silence had overcome her—the silence that seemed to underlie all the daily bustle afforded a peculiar kind of comfort. She never felt the urge to come out of it. But on the quiz contest set, someone had shrieked, "Silence!" and the entire set had fallen quiet at once. It wasn't the kind of silence to which Madhubani was accustomed. The quiz contest silence was not exactly a quiet one. Underneath were all kind of sounds that stuck to the mind like honeybees. The tick-tick sound was one that took your breath away.

Now there were new contestants on the show. A man dressed in a sanyasi's saffron robes was there to give the prizes away. He was speaking the kind of English one heard in English movies. It was clear that his mustache was dyed. Her father was standing next to a man, his arms folded in a pleading posture. Signaling to him that she would be back in a minute, Madhubani climbed the steps that took her out of the basement.

Outside, there were other sounds. In the narrow lawn in front of the hospital, the relatives of patients were sprawled, one hand under the head, the other holding a newspaper. An assistant director from the TV channel, who had been prowling on the sets with a cap crookedly balanced on her head and scrawling something on a pad, had taken a cigarette break and was puffing away with great concentration as though she were performing pranayama. Except for the Rajasthani women who worked as construction laborers in her hometown, Madhubani had never seen a woman smoke before. Remembering Mona Darling in Hindi movies standing next to the villain with a cigarette in her hand, she saw features of the vamp in the assistant director. The cigarette didn't go with the big bindi on the girl's forehead, but it did go with her jeans. It didn't suit her bangles and anklets, but did suit her decisive posture. She was blowing the smoke straight to heaven through the curls on her forehead.

Observing Madhubani staring at her, the girl jumped up and asked: "How are you feeling now? Better?" Then she said: "Oh, I shouldn't smoke here. It's a hospital, isn't it?" She threw away the cigarette, and gave Madhubani a peppermint even as she popped one into her own mouth as she ran inside. Madhubani was pleased at how quickly the vamp had morphed into a heroine. She even liked the faint whiff of smoke clinging to the girl.

As Madhubani moved toward the hospital canteen, people stopped her to ask: "Which way is the drugstore?" "Which way is the Emergency Ward?" "Where does one register?" "Will the blood bank be open now?"

There was an information booth nearby, staffed by a woman wearing pink lipstick, giving directions in a raised voice. Depending on the clothes of those who approached her, the woman's voice rose and fell accordingly. In the drugstore, people with quavering voices asked questions like "Don't you have a less expensive drug? Wouldn't it do to take just one injection?"

Those who waited on the bench asked: "Was that your daughter who stayed here last night?"

"Will your patient be discharged tomorrow?"

"Has your son taken leave from office?"

There was a strange way in which to answer these questions—to unburden oneself. But inside, under the spotlights, the questions were:

"What is this strain of penicillin called?"

"Is euthanasia legal in India?"

"Which Indian Olympic medalist is today living in a Kolkata slum?"

Even when Madhubani knew the answers, these questions were terrifying. Here, even if there were no answers, there was no fear. No, she couldn't go back to the quiz.

As though entering a familiar place, Madhubani went into the canteen. The seat where Buddhooram had been was empty. It was as though he had just gone out and would be back again soon. Although Madhubani wanted to sit at the same table as before, there was already a middle-aged woman there. She seemed as if she were quietly drinking a cup of tea, but she was actually sobbing to herself. She kept wiping her cheeks with the tissues on the table, sucking the tea in as though she was breathing intermittently with every sip that fueled her private journey—like the assistant director who drew in the smoke of her cigarette so intensely. The woman was wetting the tissues with her tears, while Buddhooram had made a boat of the same tissue for Kareena Kapoor's river of moonlight. Madhubani felt like going up to the woman and sitting close to her, touching her—in Buddhooram's place.

Sohanlal came looking for his daughter. Shaking her a little, he said, "Come on, come on. Eat something. They will call you in for the four p.m. session. It was quite a job to persuade that production chap."

Madhubani froze. "No, Papa, I can't do it."

"What!" uttered Sohanlal.

"What's so great in giving them the answers I've learned by heart? Those people who ask questions or give prizes haven't heard of Jyotsna Bhabhi and Sejal, have they? Fifteen thousand people died in Bhopal, not just four! Three lakh people are still suffering. What does that man know about all this? It's merely a quiz question for him. I don't want any of this . . ." She started walking briskly away along the corridor.

"Stop, stop!" cried Sohanlal.

They had to step aside so that a gurney could be wheeled past into the ICU. A nurse, holding a glucose bottle and feeling the patient's pulse, was saying, "Quick, quick."

Sohanlal caught Madhubani's hand and made her sit down on the white bench outside the ICU. Several people were sitting around waiting to be sent on an errand by anyone coming out of the ICU. Madhubani felt bad that she couldn't see the face of the man who was taken in, wondering miserably if it was Buddhooram. The bench they sat on was made of old wood, and had grown smooth with people sitting on it. Sohanlal took Madhubani's hand, and said, "Don't be stubborn. Come, make up your mind."

Madhubani's mind was inside the ICU. Was it Buddhooram behind the frosted glass? If that was so, were his relatives here? She began to look around. It seemed as though the people were looking at her own father with concern. So she turned to him, and realized he was sobbing quietly, with his hands covering his face. She tried to pull his hands away, and shook him gently. Those next to them indicated to her soundlessly that she should let him be.

After weeping for five minutes, Sohanlal muttered, "I'll show them, I'll show our townspeople . . . why I ran away fifty years ago . . . show them . . ." He began to sob again.

"Now what happened? Come, let's go have lunch," said his daughter.

"They said I had stolen something and run away. I was very young then, Madhu. Then they spread the rumor that I was a smuggler in Ankleshwar. Then they said I was in jail. Arre! Just because a person is not around anymore doesn't mean that everyone can bad-mouth him. Destroy him in their minds. No one wanted anything good to happen to me. Do they know with what difficulty I've built a life? I'll show them . . . Let them see my daughter on TV. I've led a respectable life. Let them see how I've brought up my daughter so that people can applaud her. Madhu, you have to answer the world's questions in front of everyone. You have to win a prize. Then the whole world will look at you. The townspeople will see you too. They'll see me, too, on TV, in the audience. Then everyone will know. Please . . . Madhu . . . please . . ." said Sohanlal, holding her hand. Without hearing what he was saying, the expressions of the people around them seemed to only suggest that the patient would get well and he shouldn't worry.

Not knowing how to comfort her father, Madhubani merely said, "Theek, Papa, sure." She made him get up and go to the canteen with her. They ordered rice plates. Sohanlal took the puris, papad, and gulab jamun from his plate and piled them onto Madhubani's. *How can I lessen his pain? How can I quieten his turmoil?* wondered Madhubani. The father who had encouraged her to study day and night, who worked overtime in the factory to save money for this trip, who begged and pleaded with the production manager these last two hours, the bile that had aged him prematurely . . . how it had all come out while sitting on that bench outside the ICU. She realized it would be impossible to tell him that it was fifty years ago and no one cared anymore about anything in his hometown. That place was nowhere but in his own mind. That was what had provoked him to work so hard and brought him to where he was now. How could she tell him that they needn't live by other people's standards? As though it was the only way she could make him happy, she asked him in a lively voice, "Papa, what was the amount first decided as compensation for the Bhopal victims?"

Like a man with a new lease of life, Sohanlal pulled a small old blue diary from his pocket and started thumbing through the pages.

"First finish your lunch, Papa, and then tell me," said Madhubani.

"Here, the jamun's really nice. You should eat half. After we finish eating, let's go over all the questions again. Exactly at four p.m. we have to go inside," said Sohanlal seriously.

Madhubani sat on the lawn and went through the diary. Her father's helpless esteem for her had once again skewed her attitude toward the world of questions. Suddenly Sohanlal shouted, "Buddhooram!"

He was standing near the hospital's main entrance, examining a statue that was there. Hearing Sohanlal's voice, he signaled to both of them to come closer. Madhubani ran to him, and Sohanlal followed her.

"Still haven't finished your quiz? Look here . . . this is the statue of a man called Nanavati who set up this hospital. See how nice the stone is? See how well made it is? But here's a quiz question for you. Are the spectacles on the statue real? Don't you feel like putting a finger through it to see if there is glass or not? Isn't it funny? A stone statue with real glasses!" Buddhooram laughed heartily.

Madhubani also found it odd. The glasses of this seemingly eternal statue seemed ephemeral.

"There are people who steal such things too. The Gandhi statue in the town square also doesn't escape the thieves. Maybe the really big statues don't have to worry."

"Whatever you say, the glasses look quite funny, no?" Then he went on, "Okay, ask your quizmaster this question. Are the spectacles on a statue real or fake? Four options: A. Fake; B. Real; C. Three-fourths fake; D. Three-fourths real." Buddhooram laughed.

Both father and daughter found his laughter beautiful. Madhubani felt like stroking his cheek. As though fulfilling her wish, Sohanlal patted Buddhooram's cheek. "For that last round, she needs your good wishes. We've come from far away," he said.

"Even the moonlight comes from a distant town," said Buddhooram. "And once it gets here, tell me where she lives. Quick . . . Tick . . . tick . . . tick . . ."

"I know the answer," said Madhubani.

"Great," said Buddhooram. Then he observed the doctors coming on their rounds and said, "Baap re! I'm finished!" He dashed into the elevator, limping a bit as he ran. Until the doors closed on him, he kept laughing luminously. Because one leg of his hospital pajamas seemed shorter than the other, it gave him a mischievous air.

The father and daughter went down the steps into the basement and inside the studio. The rules were announced. The spot boys made way for Madhubani with compassion. The quizmaster was not to be seen. Sohanlal was made to sit in the audience next to a woman in a blue sari. He sat, smiling and waving a hand at his daughter. Just then the quizmaster came out from the makeup room wearing a new coat like a bridegroom. But his yellow tie had been swung onto his shoulder during the makeup session, and he had forgotten to reposition it. This made him look a little comic. The tie was on his back, funny—like the statue's glasses. Who would tell him? How would he ever come to know?

"Silence." Everyone sat quietly. Madhubani was made to stand on the side of the set, being told to go up to her place on the stage when called. In the darkness, standing in that strange silence, Madhubani took out the paper boat from her purse. Holding it in her palm, slowly closing her eyes, she prayed in earnest: "God, please let Kareena come." The small paper boat carrying all the weight of the world started moving forward in the moonlight, tenderly.

"Tik Tik Geleya," 2004

NO PRESENTS PLEASE

THE HALF-FINISHED GHATKOPAR FLYOVER, OR OVERPASS, looked like a bridge that had been bombed. The iron spikes of the columns between the unfinished stretches on either side seemed to be piercing the sky, which could be seen trapped in between. Below, the vehicles crawled their way through the construction rubble and slowly disappeared. This was the fate of all roads. A man could stop wherever he wanted, but a road?

By the side of such a road, holding a large album wrapped in plastic, twenty-two-year-old Popat stands, distraught. His fiancé, Asavari Lokhande, who works in the ball pen factory on the opposite side of the road, is about to appear on a one-hour break. In the album are samples of wedding invitations. He has borrowed it from a friend who works in a printing press. Popat and Asavari have to choose one from these samples and have the card printed today, in anticipation of their wedding. That is why Popat has gone on the night shift.

Asavari was never late. As the cloud of cement dust from two passing trucks settled, she emerged from it as if in a dream sequence from a film, waving her hand. Her hair was so tightly tied in a bun that no truck's slip-stream could loosen it. Her eyes were sparkling, quite unaffected by the dust. Popat held up the album for her to see, looked to either side, and dashed across the road as though he were swimming, clutching the album to his chest.

Even the dry afternoon breeze seemed refreshing to Asavari. "So you brought it," she said happily. There was a domesticity in her voice that appealed to Popat; it was as if she had said, "Did you bring the rice and dal?"

"We don't have much time. Have to decide soon. Let's sit somewhere here." Popat looked around for a seat, and led Asavari through the rows of huge stone slabs meant for use in the flyover. There was a bit of shade cast by one of the slabs. The silence of the hot afternoon included the sounds of the passing trucks, the mixers churning the pebbles and concrete, and the local trains passing every minute at Kanjurmarg Station nearby.

Sitting down on a pockmarked stone, Asavari took the album from Popat and began leafing through it. He saw the sweat on her slender neck and felt more intimate toward her. As she turned the pages, colorful mock-ups of invitations scrolled by. None of them had any text. Looking at them, Asavari was frightened. These empty wedding invitations without any writing looked like the empty municipal housing board flats that no one went to live in, like empty wedding halls. As she looked silently at the samples, Popat said, "Look at this one. The bouquets of flowers, the touch of haldi-kumkum— looks quite real. It's done through screenprinting." He helped Asavari turn the heavy pages. "This sort of expensive thing is not for us" was the undercurrent of his words.

For Asavari, the album seemed like a bundle of countless possibilities. All sorts of weddings and all sorts of families lay inside, as did the sounds of all kinds of orchestras and brass bands. But it wasn't difficult to find a few simple and inexpensive varieties—they were all in the last section of the album. Both of them liked a card in pale pink. On either side was a small fold, with a line drawing of a pair of birds. "This one is fine," said Popat with pride, shaking Asavari's hand.

Asavari slipped the card out of its plastic folder and held it in her hand.

"Hey, it will get dirty. Put it back in. My friend at the press gave me the album. No customer gets such special treatment. Put it back, put it back!" jabbered Popat.

Asavari slapped his head lightly and said, "Shut up!"

On the bridge above, a truck raised its rear and poured out a load of sand. Below, the two sat amid the stones, gazing with concentration at the pale pink card. The card looked back at them, giving them a small fright, as though it hid a mysterious secret about their future wedded life. Scenes flashed past: drinking sugarcane juice together; walking through lonely parks talking loving nonsense; her wanting to travel in the ladies' compartment and his insisting on her coming into the general, and putting his arm around her in that hostile crowd; her making a scene at the bus stop, saying that she wouldn't marry him if he wore a safari suit; her walking out of the shop where a salesman had taunted him with earrings way beyond his budget, her saying they were not good enough for the price, and thus freeing him from a spell. These scattered images were now going to be tied together by a heavy rope, the pink card mirroring this merciless law of society. Like a closed fortress door, the card seemed to be telling them: "Look," "Think."

If they counted all their friends on both sides, the number would probably be a hundred. But even if they printed only a hundred invitations, they would still have to pay for three hundred, which is why the friend at the press had told them that they might as well print the higher number. A serious problem faced them: what would they do with the remaining cards, who would they give them to? It was possible that they could increase their circle of friends and relatives by giving out the cards to the panwala, the istriwala, the guard in the park, the boys who stood at signals selling stale flowers they took from yesterday's arrangements in the big hotels. All the people one knew over the years without knowing them, or knew but did not really know, those who smiled from beyond a Lakshman rekha. With the card, they might come wearing ironed clothes, cross the line, shake hands with the bride and groom, and go back across the line again. The working women might start leaving their small children in their rented rooms. They might get invited to other people's weddings.

Wearing new clothes, you might change buses and trains, sit yawning on metal folding chairs in a tent somewhere amid strangers, have other strangers ladling food onto your plate, take a mug of water from another stranger to wash your hands, chew your betel leaf and nut, and leave quietly without saying goodbye to anyone. So who was kin and friend, and who was not?

The shadow of the broken bridge moved eastward with the sun. Asavari and Popat stood up and walked to the kala-khatta vendor who stood beyond a heap of construction pebbles. They asked for a "by-two." Popat was of the firm belief that a "by-two" yielded more of the beverage than one full glass. Asavari shrieked that she didn't want ice. She believed that the more ice there was, the less juice the glass held. As they drained the last drops, the vendor looked at them mischievously, thinking they were secret lovers searching for privacy, and waved at a nearby junkyard filled with old cement mixers: "You can go there if you like. I'll keep an eye out for anyone coming this way."

Asavari's face burned, as though something in the atmosphere was mocking the pink wedding card. She drank up the juice, put down her glass, and said, "Let's go to the platform," and started walking briskly toward Kanjurmarg Station through a shortcut. Feeling that the card had the power to lift them from filth, Asavari sat down on the cement bench on platform three and started drafting the text of the invitation on a piece of paper she found in her purse.

Popat had run after her, clutching the album to his chest. He now stood panting, watching her write out the words. Her pen shook in the breeze, and seemed to have stopped in embarrassment. It was customary for the elders, the parents, to invite the wedding guests. This was what they had seen on invitation cards. But these two, without a past, born from the city's navel and raised by the city, did not know what to do now. They did not know who their parents were. They could not even think of anyone they could name as elders or well-wishers. Asavari cast her thoughts to the khaki-clad women in the remand home in Chembur. Popat thought of the old Parsi gentleman who gave him an extra four annas when he used to polish shoes opposite Churchgate Station. Asavari felt deflated. Popat looked into space.

Popat had first seen her when he had got a "temp" job for six months at the ball pen factory. She worked deftly in the department that separated bad ball pens from good. When the supervisor sometimes shouted at her, the other girls who giggled with her and shared their lunch boxes maintained their distance and acted more involved in their tasks, seemingly unconnected to her public humiliation. This had caused Popat a lot of pain. As she had seen this pain in his helpless eyes, their worlds had united.

Looking unseeingly at a local train passing by, Popat said, "Just our names will do. Hurry up and write. And no Marathi or Hindi. My friends don't know Marathi. Write in English. You know how to."

"No, I will get Varsha Madam to write it for me."

"No, no, it has to be ready in half an hour. Write it yourself. Then I'll get the bookseller on the platform, Mr. Tripathi, to check it for mistakes."

Placing the piece of paper on the album, Asavari started writing in English: "We invite you to our wedding reception at Phanaswadi Chawl on . . ." Then she shook her head and scratched through the sentence. Suddenly she wrote: "Popat marries Asavari Lokhande," then scratched it out and wrote, "Asavari Lokhande marries Popat." Either way it sounded like one was doing the other a favor. She went back to writing "We are getting married, etc. . . ." and then wrote their names below, hers to the right and Popat's to the left. Seeing the names together for the first time on this little piece of paper in Roman letters, Asavari shivered, feeling as though they were submitting themselves to a sanctified social structure.

Suddenly she placed both her hands on her ears, closed her eyes, and sobbed, internalizing this moment. Having moved closer to her on the bench, Popat looked at her intently. A home, a kitchen with pots and pans, a garland on the door, feast days, toothbrush, soap, curtains—the lucky few who had all these and alongside whom he had walked on the street—a life he never thought they would have had suddenly been brought close to them by the scribbled text of an invitation card.

Asavari continued to keep her eyes shut. Popat looked at the paper in her hand and read the words aloud. "Asavari Lokhande." Compared with this solid name, his own—Popat—looked trashy. Somehow this didn't seem fair. Something was not in order. Two boys with a slender ladder were pasting cinema posters in separate pieces on the hoardings on the platform. Feeling cheated, Popat said, "Your name is so sturdy. And it has a surname too. Seems like the name of a posh family. Mine is nothing in front of yours. It's not even a man's name. In your Marathi, *Popat* means a parrot, doesn't it? I'm an ordinary parrot . . ."

"Cheh," said Asavari. "How stupid you are. It's a name given to you lovingly, isn't it?"

He grabbed her hand. "Lovingly, my foot. It's a useless name. Anyway, what caste is your name?"

Asavari was shocked. This was not language he had ever used. This was language unrelated to them.

She was a street orphan picked up by a van and brought to the remand home in Chembur. A woman called Lokhandebai used to teach the kids songs and prayers in the remand home. When she played the harmonium, a child used to sit very close to her and sing intensely as though her vocal cords would burst. Lokhandebai called her Asavari; it was supposed to be the name of a raga. Even after the teacher left, everyone in the remand home continued to call the girl "Miss Lokhandebai's Asavari," and so her name became Asavari Lokhande. The indistinct memory of the woman with her soft touch, clad in a pale yellow sari, who seemed like the mother she had never seen, stayed with Asavari only because of the name that was now hers and which she had seen no reason to discard. She had told Popat this story at least a hundred times. But in this impersonal public moment, she could not see how to console Popat for his distress at the sight of her last name. Frightened at how the draft invitation had changed his

very language, she scratched out her surname and instantly felt unburdened. She looked at him, as if to say
"Happy?"

"It's Mumbai that has fed us and raised us. We
shouldn't offend Mumbai by taking on random people's
names," said Popat in a defeated voice.

In front of them thousands of names went to and fro
in the trains. Looking at the flood of people coming out
of the trains, Popat said, "See Asavari, look at the fake
good fortune of these bastards. Each one of them knows
his caste. Because each one of them knows who their
parents are. Now, see how they go hither and thither
holding their caste in their hands, as though they'd
stolen it . . . We don't need to bother with all that, do
we?" He began to laugh loudly. Asavari got up, saying
she was getting late.

Mr. Tripathi of the curly gray hair, owner of the
platform bookstall, wrote out the invitation draft afresh
for them in his clear handwriting. Casting a happy
glance at the couple, he joked, "Have you looked for a
kholi to rent, or are you planning to set up house on the
last bench on platform number three?"

While he was writing out the invitation, his lower
lip twisted a little to one side, and Asavari asked, "Nowadays people write 'Your blessings are our gift' and 'No
presents please'—should we write those too?"

"That's a rich-people style, my daughter," said

Tripathi. "That's not for us. If anyone gives you something lovingly, don't refuse it. Yours is a new household, you'll need everything. All the best to you," he said, handing over the piece of paper.

They both felt that he was wishing them on behalf of the entire world, and felt like touching his feet. But they were hidden deep inside his stall, behind the rows of magazines. Not knowing what else to do, they sketched a bow. Understanding what they meant, Tripathi said, "Jeete raho, live long." As they both turned to leave, Tripathi shouted after them, "Arre, Popat, your name doesn't look so good on the invitation card. Get a new name. Naya naam, nayi zindagi— new name, new life."

The two climbed up onto the iron bridge of the station and stood, holding on to the grille. From here they could see all three platforms. On the rails lay the afternoon sun, as if unaware of the trains about to run over him. Suddenly, Popat turned into a spinning top. His entire world was standing on tiptoe, begging for a new name. "What Tripathi said was right, Asavari. This is my only chance. Quick, quick, give me a new name," he said excitedly.

Asavari stroked his back and said, "Cheh . . ."

"No, no. No cheh or chih. Hurry, look for a name. It'll make everything new. Everything will change. Nothing stylish, nothing fancy . . . just give me a new name . . . hurry . . . We have to give the printer the card before three o'clock. Hurry!" said Popat, tugging her arm.

Asavari did not know what to think. A train drew into the station and deposited thousands of names at their feet. How many different kinds of names there were, each with its distinct features, clothing, memories, scent, its own heaven and hell. Popat shook her. "Swapnil? Yes? How's Swapnil? I heard that name on TV once. Write it down . . . hurry. Swapnil. Get the spelling from Tripathi if you like," he said, trembling with excitement. He looked like someone hanging on to the wings of a plane at the very last moment, after it had already taken flight.

Frightened that her entire beloved universe was being destroyed by this scrap of an invitation, Asavari held his shoulders with both her hands. "What's happened to you, Popat? Everything's fine, Popat. Aren't you my own Popat?" She spoke softly. His eyes, searching for a new name, looked quite different than the way she knew them. She felt she had to save things from destruction right now. Perhaps it could be done only by tearing up the draft invitation. She tore the invitation, crumpled the pieces into a ball, and swung her arm to throw it away. At the last minute, as though it were a sacred flower given to her from someone's puja, she held herself back and put away the ball of paper inside her purse. Popat had been staring in astonishment, waiting to see where the paper ball would fall. In that moment, the distant half-finished overpass, the iron spikes, the faraway trucks, the construction rubble, the approaching trains, all looked like children's toys to Popat.

"No Presents Please," 2000

TRANSLATOR'S NOTE

Undertaking this translation was for me a coming to terms with the ruse of the ordinary that Jayant Kaikini has mastered. While "ruse" is often understood as subterfuge or deception, I read it as a gentle narrative trick, so evident in every single story of this collection. The trick, then, is to begin with an extremely "ordinary" person or situation, sometimes both—a middle-aged bachelor, a married couple growing indifferent to each other, a mischievous little boy terrorizing his neighbors. Gradually, as the story unfurls, the bachelor is plunged into commotion over a marriage proposal and his very connection to the city changes; the couple's apartment is occupied by a girlfriend who becomes close to the wife; the little boy is taken away to be put into a remand home in Bombay. The ordinary often reveals itself as surreal—as it does when the mirrors come to life with the bachelor's inner turmoil, the two women become a two-headed, four-breasted creature that drives out the man of the house, and the little boy copes with chawl life and cats howling in cages.

The challenge for me, then, was to maintain the ordinariness of the narrative until it could be maintained no longer, and to let the translation lead the reader along without drawing attention to itself. At the same time, when the surreal began to seep into the story, and the ruse of the ordinary opened out onto a different terrain of engagement for the characters, the translation had to find the right words to signal this "turn."

I am not a prolific translator and I don't usually take up commissions. I translate something if I can make it my own, something I'm also personally invested in. And I've always been invested in Jayant Kaikini's stories, both for their brilliance of technique and the obsession with Bombay, which mirrored mine. The first time I engaged intensely with his work was when I translated his poetry into English in the late 1970s, and I feel that something of the kind of engagement poetry requires has come into this translation as well, in terms of the mode of translation. It is worth recalling here that Jayant was originally a poet who became a fiction writer. His fiction captures some of the economy of modern Kannada poetry in phrase and structure, and I would like to think my translation has tried to do the same thing. Through the translation of his fiction, I'm invoking the past of our old connection with poetry, so that somehow the old connection and the new are talking to each other.

We selected the stories together, but I kept pushing for my favorite ones. We had a debate over retranslating some stories that had already appeared in print. There were three of those—"Dagadu Parab's Wedding Horse," "Unframed," and "Mogri's World." Since I couldn't visualize an anthology of Jayant's fiction in English without these iconic stories, I have taken the liberty of translating them once more so as to match the language and style of the rest of the stories. The translations in this book were done in many places, several of them in Bombay. There was always a special thrill to working on them during my regular Bombay visits. I'd be traveling in a local train and suddenly I'd think of something and send Jayant an SMS to which he'd reply instantly. Sometimes I would find myself in places such as Flora Fountain, the Gateway of India, Opera House, or the deepest suburbs, and look at them through Jayant's characters: wasn't that Mogri clinging to the handrail in the women's compartment of the Churchgate–Borivali slow train, wasn't that Paali getting into a boat at the Gateway, wasn't that Kunjbihari leaning out of his taxi at the airport, and wasn't that Dagadu with the horses on Juhu Beach?

As an outsider to Bombay myself, I probably see the city with the same affection and curiosity that Jayant displays. That's also the special bond I have with the stories—which are about somewhat displaced people, they aren't the local elite, they aren't even long-term residents, many of them are migrants or drifters. We know that since the beginnings of Bombay's rise as a metropolis, more than 80 percent of the population was born outside the city. And that makes for a very unique cityscape. So, there's a stability to Bombay—perhaps the shape of the buildings, the settledness of its urbanity—and at the same time there's a deep instability because of the constant coming and going of people. Jayant has been going back for nearly forty years, and I perhaps for a little less, but there's always something recognizable about the city, like Jayant's anecdote, and those of so many others, about the auto driver who will give him back two rupees as change even after a ride at midnight. That sense of being both insider and outsider in relation to Bombay that Jayant and I share is one of the reasons for the bond between writer and translator.

I began working on the translations with a sense of relief that the writer was not using a little-known dialect and that the writing seemed, at first glance, not to pose any problems of comprehension. A friend had likened Jayant's style to the idea of Roland Barthes's white writing. How this would translate in our context is that the writing is not colored by ethnic or regional origin. Most other Kannada writers, on the other hand, do "color" their writing. Curiously, my father, the novelist Niranjana, whose work I have translated and who would perhaps not have shared anything with Jayant except the fascination with Bombay, wrote prose in a particular way in the 1960s as a deliberate modernist gesture. For him, the concern was to overcome the caste markers of his protagonists by making the writing plain. His style was to work with short sentences and plainness of speech. To always choose the Kannada word over the Sanskrit word. I actually find elements of that deliberate plainness in Jayant's writing. But here the difference is that the writing is also trying to deal with a situation where the characters are not speaking Kannada although their dialogue is being reported to us in the language.

The difficulty was to retain in my translation the flavor of the speech, the hybrid Hindi-Urdu-Dakhani speech that is the cultural vernacular of Bombay and is signaled prominently in all the stories. In the flow of plain Kannada writing, these hybrid phrases are signposts that function in such a way as to mark, in Ashish Rajadhyaksha's phrase, a sort of territorial realism. Jayant and I argued about how much of this to translate into English. After he complained about my frugality, I put back some of the phrases I'd removed or translated out. But I also worried about the book that we were setting adrift in the world, away from Bombay, and the fact that it would acquire readers without proficiency in Hindustani. I solved that problem by doing parallel translations—leaving in the Hindustani word but giving the meaning in English either close by or else-where in the sentence so that the attentive reader even-tually understands the meaning. This way, nothing goes completely unexplained, even as the public language of the city makes itself heard in the sentences.

The fascinating mismatch between Jayant's protag-onists and the language they speak in the fiction leads us to a seemingly unrelated issue, thinking about which might tell us more about the relative lack of Kannada critical writing on his work. Like the eminent play-wright Girish Karnad, Jayant is also a Konkani speaker who writes in Kannada, but this does not completely explain the lack of attention paid to his fiction. The cul-tural theorist Ashwin Kumar has remarked that there are very few Kannada writers who don't think of them-selves as public intellectuals. As important as the fact that they are novelists is the fact that they are social crit-ics. Jayant's own personality is such that he has not been politically involved in the context of Karnataka. But if we attempt to explain this outside the frame of indi-vidual preference, an explanation with limited weight, we may want to note that in what Jayant's stories talk about, we cannot see any automatic constituency that he represents or speaks for. One cannot be a represen-tative of these "riff-raff" migrants who are the major-ity of Jayant's characters because they are not a unified linguistic constituency. Since, in India, we have literary formation, linguistic formation, and political formation all coming together, the writer as public intellectual is one who speaks from out of this combined formation. Hence, although Jayant writes in Kannada, people may wonder if he is a "Kannada writer." The language of Jayant Kaikini's fiction—as well as the characters who populate the stories—exceed the post-Independence dynamic that ties language to identity. In doing this, they speak to the experience of the city that smoulders in these pages.

I give thanks to Tanveer Hasan, who offered me indispensable multilingual advice.

Tejaswini Niranjana
Bangalore, April 2016

© Dinesh Shenoy

JAYANT KAIKINI is a Kannada poet, short story writer, columnist, and playwright, as well as an award-winning lyricist and script and dialogue writer for Kannada films. He won his first Karnataka Sahitya Akademi Award at the age of nineteen in 1974 and has since won the award three times, in addition to winning various other awards in India, including the first Kusumagraj Rashtriya Bhasha Sahitya Puraskar. Born in the coastal temple town Gokarn, Kaikini lived in Mumbai for two decades before moving to Bangalore, where he now lives. His latest book is a collection of essays on cinema. *No Presents Please*, his volume of selected stories, is the first book in translation to have won the DSC Prize for South Asian Literature.

TEJASWINI NIRANJANA won the Central
Sahitya Akademi Award for best translation for M. K. In-
dira's *Phaniyamma* (1989) and the Karnataka Sahitya Aka-
demi Award for her translation of Niranjana's *Mrityunjaya*
(1996). She has also translated Pablo Neruda's poetry and
Shakespeare's *Julius Caesar* into Kannada. Her transla-
tions into English include Vaidehi's *Gulabi Talkies* (2006).
She grew up in Bangalore and has studied and worked in
Mumbai. She is currently professor of cultural studies at
Lingnan University, Hong Kong.